THE
GOOD WORKS
OF
AYELA LINDE

THE
GOOD WORKS
OF
AYELA LINDE

A NOVEL IN STORIES

CHARLOTTE FORBES

ARCADE PUBLISHING • NEW YORK

FIRST EDITION

This is a work of fiction. Names, places, characters, and incidents are either products of the author's imagination or are used fictitiously.

An earlier version of "Parasols" appeared in *Narrative Magazine* in 2004. An earlier version of "The Marvelous Yellow Cage" appeared in *Glimmer Train Stories* in 2004 and as part of the anthology *Where Love Is Found*, published by Washington Square Press in 2006.

Library of Congress Cataloging-in-Publication Data

Forbes, Charlotte.
  The good works of Ayela Linde : a novel in stories / by Charlotte Forbes. —1st ed.
     p. cm.
  ISBN 1-55970-807-7 (alk. paper)
  I. Title.

PS3606.O69G66 2006
813'.6—dc22   2005029294

Published in the United States by Arcade Publishing, Inc., New York
Distributed by Time Warner Book Group

Visit our Web site at www.arcadepub.com

10   9   8   7   6   5   4   3   2   1

EB

PRINTED IN THE UNITED STATES OF AMERICA

For lovely Alina
and, of course,
for Joe

Contents

Acknowledgments

Many thanks . . .

To my agent, Sorche Fairbank, and my editor, Cal Barksdale, for their graciousness and excellent work. To Arcade for publishing the book, to Tessa Aye, and to everyone involved in its production — Lynn Buckley for the jacket design, Roland Ottewell for copyediting, and Miranda Ottewell for proofreading. To members of my writing group, Karen, Sarah, Joyce, Susan, Patsy, Ruchama, and Cynthia, for their encouragement and insightful comments on these stories. To my friends Linda Stallone, Fran Siegel, and Rose Reichman, for their willingness to read and react to my work at a moment's notice. To my husband, Joe Stallone, and my daughter, Alina, who have always given me the time to write — no questions asked.

THE
GOOD WORKS
OF
AYELA LINDE

1
Parasols
1934

You once gave me something, though I'm sure you didn't mean to.

What you gave me is hard to explain. All I can say was that it stopped the flood of my own self for a moment and left me shining inside, like summer moonlight.

It happened the year we were seventeen and I was new to your tiny town of Santa Rosalia, north of the Rio Grande.

Everyone had said to stay away from you. "That girl is a hard one," they said, "and a round heels too," which in those days meant a girl who went down easy for a boy.

That's just what I wanted to learn from you, how to be hard and easy at once.

I didn't know there was anything else to know.

Then on that stifling Saturday I let you tell your mama you were staying the night at my house.

"Where should I tell my mama I'm staying?" I asked you.

You looked beyond me. "Wherever you want."

I shut my eyes and saw my papa's face collapse and Mama's tears run down her cheeks if they found us out.

Still, I went with you.

You were working when I came for you. Both you and your mother, Felidia Garzón, sewing in worlds of your own.

No one came when I jingle-jangled the bells to the dress shop. I had to walk through the empty shop to the workroom, and there you were, dear Ayela. Sitting on a high stool, bent over your sewing, stitching your mother's leftover scraps onto the old parasols you got from anywhere you could.

Felidia Garzón had the ears of a dog. "Hello Druanne," she greeted me without looking up from her Singer machine. "What will you girls do at your house on such a hot night?"

Before words came to me, you spoke. "We're going to pray, Mother. We're going to pray to God to make it Sunday so we can go to church and pray some more."

Felidia Garzón frowned. "I was speaking to Druanne." She finished the seam and tore the thread with her teeth. "Why don't you girls stay here and help me cut patterns? I could put the two of you to good use."

You hopped down from the stool and put your sewing things in the basket and lined the parasol you were working on up against the far wall with all the others.

"We're going now," you said.

Felidia Garzón went right on with what she was doing. "Mass is at nine-thirty tomorrow morning," she said. "And don't take breakfast or you can't receive Communion."

You didn't reply. Without bothering to change your dress or kiss your mother good-bye, you walked out of the workroom.

Felidia Garzón stopped me. Why didn't we stay with her next Saturday night?

We could listen to the Victrola, have some nougats. "I'm not such an ogre," she said.

"No, señora," I mumbled, my eyes on the floor for fear they might expose our lie.

You appeared in the doorway. "Are you coming?" you asked with startling impatience.

Bless you, I wanted to cry. "You are my true savior!"

But when we were alone on the street you turned on me: "God in heaven, Druanne, what did you do to your face?"

My hand went to my cheek, and remembered. "It's Mama's makeup," I mumbled. "I had to put it on fast, without the mirror. So she wouldn't know."

You laughed that hard laugh of yours. "You schoolgirls, you think that's what it's all about."

You didn't even have the decency to watch me blush.

You were glaring at the steaming evening that had come to suffocate us all. With a sigh you took a small fan out of your bodice. "It's too hot to live," you said, and fanned yourself with a sour look on your face.

"Come on. Let's go," I begged. "Damaso Montell is going to be there tonight! Do you hope Gabriel Frank is there?"

You said you didn't care.

"Or Roberto Solere?"

You didn't reply, so I asked again.

"It's all the same," you said, turning the corner on Obispo Street.

I skipped to keep up with you. "Damaso Montell will be

there. I saw him outside the hotel this afternoon in his waiter's uniform. He told me he'd be there."

You kept walking. "Damaso Montell is an oaf. An oaf who can't hold his liquor."

"If Damaso Montell is there and he asks me to dance and then takes me out by the hills, it will be the most beautiful thing in the world."

"There is nothing beautiful in this world," you said in a voice as flat and frightening as death.

We didn't speak again until we were across the street from the pool hall. A group of men stood smoking and talking around the entrance. You must have known they were watching you, as all men watched you wherever you went. Before we crossed the street, you touched my arm. "Wait," you said, laughing that hard laugh of yours. Then you told me a story about a traveling circus where the elephants broke loose and wandered through the town trampling the gardens and sending people screaming into their houses until the mayor and the priest and the owner of the circus organized a posse to round them up. You told it for the men. They did not hear you, but they watched you speak and saw your head draw back laughing, showing your bone-white teeth.

When they couldn't take their eyes off you, your rose-colored summer dress, your black Mexican hair, we crossed the street and walked past them as though they didn't exist. You put your arm around me and whispered in my ear something I didn't hear. I laughed because you laughed. Together we laughed so hard we nearly fell down trying to get through the door to the pool hall.

4

*　　*　　*

In back of the hall, beyond the pool tables, was an outside dance floor lit by colored lanterns. Two couples were dancing to a small band. Men just over from the other side of the Rio Grande stood around the bar, watching them. I watched them too until I turned to stare at Damaso Montell. I stared at him so that he would feel the pull of my eyes and come to me. But he didn't.

Right away Gabriel Frank came to you, carrying a cardboard box under his arm.

You looked at the box he was carrying and laughed. "So you brought me a diamond necklace," you said.

"It's the flypaper from the butcher shop." Gabriel Frank hung his head like a whipped dog.

"Mother of God, don't be so truthful," you snapped and grabbed the box from him and put it on the ground. You were disgusted, but you let yourself be led onto the dance floor. You let Gabriel Frank place his hand on your back and your bodies move together. At your first steps to the music, a loneliness so strong came over me that I had to sit down. I went to a nearby table where a man was eating tomatoes.

Gabriel Frank danced by with you in his arms. You took turns swigging on a bottle of beer. When the band played an old Mexican ballad, Gabriel Frank put his arms around your waist and his head on your shoulder like a sleepy child.

The man next to me stubbed his cigarette out in his plate. "Too green," he said, nodding toward the tomatoes. "Who can eat such tomatoes?"

I glared at him like you might have and walked across

5

the room to Damaso Montell. "Wouldn't you rather be dancing with me than jabberwalling with your friends?" I asked him.

He laughed and said, "What took you so long?"

I put my hand on the back of his neck like you did when you danced with a man, and closed my eyes and breathed in his humid, beery smell.

When I looked up again, you and Gabriel Frank were in the corner, drinking and kissing and swaying with your bodies pressed together. Even so, I saw it in your eyes: there was a distance between you that Gabriel Frank could do nothing about.

The band stopped playing, and I followed Damaso Montell up to the bar. He ordered another beer and called his friends over, fellow waiters from the hotel restaurant.

They had been drinking since dawn.

"The rich, they eat but they never tip," one complained.

"We're going to piss in their soup," another cried.

"They're too stupid to know the difference," someone else said.

Then the idea came to them: they would not serve one more plate of food to Mr. Rich Man.

Damaso Montell watched with a frozen smirk.

"Hey, come on! We'll be rich and you'll still be eating beans," they yelled at his unmoving person, swearing that they were going that very minute to shake the manager of the hotel from his iron cot and tell him to his shriveled, gray, sleep-weary face they were quitting the only job they ever had.

When they were gone, the place seemed larger and almost quiet.

"They're just drunk," I said.

I felt Damaso Montell smile.

"Stay with me," he said.

"At the bar?"

"Forever," he whispered.

I blushed and stepped back. Oh, Ayela, why couldn't you have heard him say that?

Everywhere there was Saturday night love. In the rooms above the pool hall, on the benches in the square, on the backstairs behind the moving picture theater. Even you were out there somewhere.

Damaso Montell ran with me on the path out of town to the east, and it felt like joy racing in my heart. I lay back and waited for his lips that were smooth and slippery as a river rock. We did the things that men and women do, not the big thing, but things that made us dizzy with love until Damaso Montell pulled away and lay on his back and lit a cigarette. When he finished the cigarette, he lit up another.

"What's the matter?" I asked him.

"Nothing," he said. "Nothing."

"Shh. Do you hear the stars twinkling?" I said that, or something like that, because the beer and the kissing and the lateness of the hour had got to me.

We lay dreaming and dozing until the dark began to drop away in clumps.

I wanted to tell Damaso Montell how it was, about the dark dropping away. I wanted to tell him too that God smiles on those who serve others, even if it is only as a waiter. What I really wanted to tell him was everything at once.

I said his name and waited for his eyes to twitch, for a jerk of his body.

There was nothing.

Nothing.

Then it occurred to me that Damaso Montell looked the same way in sleep as he did awake. Like someone who wanted never to hear another word.

I got up and began to run, and when I glanced back over my shoulder, all that remained was a dark shape, like a tree fallen over in the grass.

On the path back to town the thought of you came flowing back to me and I laughed to myself. I had lost you during the night, your rose-colored dress, your hand on your hip, your laugh, your sharp eyes, especially the sharp eyes. They had gone so far from me and then like breathing they were back.

I thought of you still shipwrecked in the arms of Gabriel Frank. Now I know what she knows, I told myself. But of course I didn't.

The light of dawn was all around, pink and clean with the hope of a new day, but with no one to see it.

People were in their beds, dreaming.

The ancient buildings around the square were still.

Not even the doors to the church were open. Father Anthony Maria had yet to climb the tower to ring the bell for six o'clock Mass. It was too early for even the sacristans to be preparing the altar.

Only a gray cat was licking its paws outside Mercedes Comche's milk shop.

I was walking slowly, letting the cool air sink into my skin, when I saw them.

In the middle of the square were your parasols, fifteen, twenty of them, all opened up and scattered about on the ground. They were all ruffled, from the tips of their points to their edges, all ruffled with the layers of colors as bright as dawn, just as you had made them.

The sight of them stopped me short.

You were sitting on a bench and I ran to you, saying, "They'll get dirty. You won't be able to sell them to the ladies."

I thought you had gone mad, but you turned to me with a face that seemed refreshed from sleep. "The parasols are not for them," you said quietly. Then, after a long silence: "They're not for anyone." On your face was the desire never to leave that moment. That moment of coolness rising from the ground, the town deserted but dreaming, immaculate with early morning light and in the midst of it, the parasols, a magnificent surprise.

You sat without moving, your eyes turned toward the parasols, as if there were nothing else worth seeing.

It was plain you were not going to say another word.

I sat down beside you, trying to fix in my mind exactly what you saw.

Then I forgot about you.

I looked at the parasols for a long time.

How long we sat there I can't say. The dance hall, its beery smoky smell, the fallen tree of Damaso Montell, my horrible need for you, Mama's worried face, the feeling that nothing would ever happen, all that was wiped clean away.

Everything left me for those moments but the sight of the parasols.

I looked at them until they didn't look like parasols at all but like a flock of strange and lovely birds that had flown up from the jungle and touched down in Santa Rosalia on their way up to heaven.

And they were beautiful.

Even you had to admit that.

2
Flowers at Your Grave
1936

The realization that the flowers in the Church of San Lorenzo had wilted at the hour of Yermina Garzón's death stopped us cold. We felt our breath catch, imagining the trouble to follow.

The church bell had just rung three times when we looked up from dusting the pews and caught the lilies swooning all at once. "It's the August heat," Father Anthony Maria said, trying to calm us, but having been sacristans for more than forty years, we knew when something was amiss in this holy place. We grabbed our missals and fled.

On Violeta Street, we heard about Yermina Garzón.

"She took her last breath just as the three o'clock train blew its whistle," her daughter, Felidia Garzón, said, blessing herself.

Even though it was almost one hundred degrees, we felt a chill.

It occurred to us that Felidia Garzón would want her mother buried in holy ground. Holy ground! We didn't know whether to stand up straight and smile, or narrow our lips in disapproval. Yermina Garzón had grown up in the slums of a Caribbean slave port, that much we knew. We thought we had seen her on those moonless nights, with her fourteen strands of beads, one for each of her gods, quiet as a cat, face smeared with streaks of earth, slipping into the countryside. It was said she drank roosters' blood and brewed ill-smelling potions that could change a person's destiny. She knew the secrets for curing the incurable, or at least sparing them a drawn-out death. And some of us did seem to dimly recall the boy gone mad with rabies, his drinking water poisoned to bring him to a quick end.

Whether it had been the work of Yermina Garzón, we couldn't say, and we felt a sort of dry dread tug at our bellies. Holy ground, indeed. The town would never stand for that.

When we saw that Felidia Garzón had sent her daughter, Ayela, to fetch the priest to arrange the burial, a delicious sense of foreboding passed through us. Ayela Garzón was a headstrong, unsmiling girl, with untamed black hair and almond-shaped eyes, and an unsettling voluptuousness even in grief. Unlike her mother and her grandmother, she had no particular religion, save that of throwing herself away on the men at every possible chance.

We watched her walk quickly toward the square. When she turned down Obispo Street, we suspected it wasn't the priest she was after, but the lawyer, Frederick Linde. We knew all about Frederick Linde, a privileged sort from Boston who was passing through Santa Rosalia when the sight of Ayela Garzón so impressed him he abandoned his travels and pursued her as if she were his only chance for happiness.

We rather liked Frederick Linde. He had the looks of a leading man and the desire to please, we thought, of a hunting dog. But for Ayela Garzón? We shook our heads sadly at his misplaced ardor.

A few of us had seen them, that drizzly afternoon fifteen weeks ago. The driver of their hired car told us they waited endlessly for the justice of the peace to read his mail and finish his lunch before joining them together for eternity. On the way back, the driver heard Ayela Garzón — and he made it a point to use her maiden name — utter her first words as wife: to swear her husband to secrecy about the marriage for one year. "I'm only nineteen," she said. "And that's too young to throw myself away forever." Frederick Linde begged his bride to reconsider, but she looked out the window and said coldly, "Give me one good reason to change my mind," and went home to her mother's in time for the evening meal.

In the intervening weeks, perhaps Ayela Garzón had relented. Perhaps she had made peace with herself and was ready, eager even, for the dark ocean of matrimony. But back down on her words to Frederick Linde? Never. Now when we think back on the day of the death, we wonder if Ayela Garzón hadn't orchestrated what followed so that no one, least of all herself, could question her change of heart. Or was it a grander, more benevolent purpose she had in mind? One that would serve the dead and the living in the same stroke?

We were in the square at four o'clock when she arrived. She came toward us and we froze, holding our breath until she passed us by.

Others went on talking, even after they saw her.

Someone reported a pot of flowers dying on the kitchen table.

Another said a bouquet wilted right in her hands.

A third shuddered and said that it was all Yermina Garzón's doing. And, of course, the question of the burial was raised.

At the mention of her grandmother, we noticed a slight waver in Ayela Garzón's surly expression. We felt a sharp thrill when we saw that. Then we felt shame. We knew Ayela Garzón had real affection for her grandmother, that she had been loved more by her grandmother than by her own mother.

We moved off a little ways. We couldn't stop people from talking. And if we were entirely honest, we would say that the Garzóns had it coming. They had strange ways, the three of them, living above the dress shop, without men. The pagan carryings-on of the grandmother, the mother's high-style dresses that no one bought, and now that insolent girl with those arms, that throat, so disturbingly bare.

Ayela Garzón moved among the groups in the square, listening with defiance. Looking back, it was obvious that her presence had goaded us on, that those cold black eyes read what was going to happen as if it were in yesterday's newspaper.

When it was dark, we saw her go to the quarters her husband had taken just off the square to wait out his sentence. She was sobbing. Sobbing? The very idea was unlike Ayela Garzón. But love sees what it wants to see, and her husband embraced her and led her inside.

We knew what went on in that room. The smell of it floated through the town like a wave from the sea, and we stopped for a moment and closed our eyes. We grew drowsy with the salty scent of it, and felt ourselves sinking into the mists of our own horrifying longings. Even as our bodies stirred, we knew that this kind of thing was only a temporary balm. We weren't surprised when later that night one of us who lived across the square caught a glimpse of Ayela Garzón as she stepped onto the balcony as naked as the day she came into the world. She said something inaudible, but bitter, of that we were sure, and spat onto the ground below.

In the morning we took our coffee at Mercedes Comche's shop. She was sweeping the sidewalk outside, humming a Mexican ballad, when Frederick Linde came along. He asked her what she made of all the fuss. She let out a laugh that bubbled up to the heavens: "All the flowers in Santa Rosalia are dropping like flies. What do I make of it? Not a blessed thing." She pointed to a vase of orange poppies on the counter that looked as fresh as the minute they were picked. "If I live to be one hundred, I'll never understand how these things get so out of hand."

We laughed along with her and shook our heads at the silliness of the whole thing.

Frederick Linde nodded a somber hello to us and went to sit at the end of the counter, looking more abandoned than ever.

We could see how his wife's flammable nature bewitched him, so different from his own and the girls he knew in Boston. He had let on that he had been on the run from those girls and the weariness of his own soul. He talked about it freely among some of us, that he was on his way to make himself useful in some small manner to someone, on his way to the Southern Hemisphere, wanting nothing more than to be in a foreign land where they ate food he had never seen and spoke a language he didn't understand and sign himself on as a common laborer building a railroad or a dam or a road or some other man-made godsend that might just ease the burden of a harsh life for one or two souls. We could almost understand why he had forsaken his dream: that if he were to leave Ayela Garzón behind like an unturned stone, his heart would never give him a moment's peace.

In the café, they were talking again about Yermina Garzón. Calling her a whore, for letting her unmarried daughter raise her child in that house. Like a savage.

"Well, I don't know about that." Gertrudis Mier chewed on the licorice root that always hung from her mouth. "But someone ought to tie her body to the bed so she can't go around killing the flowers," she said.

"Such nonsense." Mercedes Comche raised her voice. "It should be stopped before someone gets hurt."

We saw what Mercedes Comche was up to. She moved down the counter pouring everyone a cup of coffee on the house. When she came to Frederick Linde, she stopped. It hadn't escaped her that Frederick Linde had taken a liking to Ayela Garzón. She knew that and more, and Frederick Linde knew she knew it. She stood over him with the coffeepot in her hand and bore down on him with a look as if she'd read every last thought in his brain and deemed them all unsatisfactory. "Do something," she commanded him.

All morning we watched Frederick Linde walk around the square, listening, defending, trying to ward off what people were secretly thinking. The futility of it was painful to see. Just before noon, we stood with the old people around Enrico Cruz, who sat at his checkerboard awaiting an opponent. "This is nothing," he said. "Just wait till Yermina Garzón starts making the orange trees drop over."

"The dead can't do that," Frederick Linde protested. "Can't you people listen to reason?" The despair in his voice surprised us.

"Only the dead know what they can do," Enrico Cruz replied quietly. "Their bones fill up with air, and you can't keep them down. I see them when the moon is out, floating through the sky. The men in dark suits, the women in their flowered dresses, and the children. Watching like they can't let us go." Enrico Cruz stopped to think for a minute. "Their eyes have gone a queer sort of color, like the half-light of dawn."

Frederick Linde had heard enough. Under the broad-brimmed hat he wore in the sun, his face was red. The heat had gotten to his thick northern blood and he looked beaten, as if he were in the midst of a trainwreck.

And where was Ayela Garzón? We had been so busy watching Frederick Linde, we had forgotten all about her. But just as her presence the day before, her absence on that day was intentional, designed to force the situation to its only acceptable resolution. Looking back, we can say that with almost total certainty.

Rebecca Sansone appeared in the square with a pot full of dead lilies and a look of disgust that produced a sudden silence in the crowd. She wore white gloves and a straw hat with tiny blue straw flowers; her dark blue dress was buttoned to her neck. We wondered how she could not be suffocating.

The sight of Rebecca Sansone always made us want to run the other way.

Nervously, we reminded ourselves of the facts: a few wilting flowers in August and an old lady's death.

Rebecca Sansone was already taking command of the crowd in the square. She walked up and down, examining us closely. "We are decent people here, are we not?" she asked in the pious voice of the righteous since the beginning of time. "Isn't there anyone who agrees with me?"

No one moved.

Then one hand went up tentatively. Another hand rose, then others.

A slow smile from Rebecca Sansone. "Alright then."

Before we knew it, Rebecca Sansone was leading a crowd toward the rectory.

We felt she had gone too far this time, that she had veered off in a perilous direction.

Like a long, sinuous snake, the crowd moved down Dolorosa Street.

Frederick Linde stepped out in front to block it.

Rebecca Sansone would not be deterred. "We're taking the matter to Father Anthony Maria," she told Frederick Linde.

"I don't see how he can stop the flowers from dying," he replied.

"Believe me, sir, it will not stop until Yermina Garzón is in the ground," she said. "But she will not be buried in the Cemetery of the Virgin of Guadalupe."

Frederick Linde reflected a moment. "Why is that?"

The widow looked him in the eye. "I'm a lot nearer to dying than you are, young man, and I'll be damned if I'm going to spend eternity in the same place as a witch." She walked past Frederick Linde, with the crowd behind her.

We watched as they made their way to the top of the street. We watched as Rebecca Sansone pounded on the heavy wood door until it opened, and the crowd filed past half-blind Sister Inez into the rectory.

We didn't go with the crowd, but we didn't try to stop them either. We went home to an uneasy siesta. After a while we heard them again, marching, talking, their voices rising to a shrill chant, passing under our window, then finally retreating from the square on their way, we could only imagine, down toward the house that held the body of Yermina Garzón. We drew the curtains and sat like stones in the darkness feeling regret, a deep regret, for we hadn't expected it to come to this — we had only expected, well, not this.

But, really, what could we have done? What possible difference could we have made?

As it turned out, we had been wise to do nothing.

Ayela Garzón told us herself. Or rather, Mrs. Linde, as she corrected us. We spotted her a few days later buying oranges at the market. Timidly, we inquired about her grandmother. "Oh, that. My husband took care of it," she said and brushed past us with an air of importance.

We learned the rest from the orange sellers.

They told us about the recent afternoon on which a man, a man with trouble chasing him, they said, bought their whole truckload of fruit. But he didn't want the fruit, they couldn't get over that. What he wanted was the use of their truck and their help in the grim business of burying the dead.

They dug a hasty gravesite, so hasty the man had strained his back. Then they went for the old woman. She was as light as a child, they told us, and died with a patient expression on her face. There was not even a pine box, they wrapped her in a blue blanket and laid her in the back of the truck. The orange sellers had sat on one side, and the daughter and granddaughter, they supposed it was, sat on the other. The daughter cried and cried, but there was something triumphant in the face of the granddaughter.

The burial was the longest and shortest they had ever known. They waited like outlaws in the truck under a stand of trees on the Olaca road. Hours passed. Toward twilight the priest appeared from nowhere. Only when it began to be dark did they drive into the cemetery.

The priest gave the order to extinguish the headlights. Uneasily, as if God were watching, he got out of the truck and read a psalm that ended so quickly it confused everyone. Then he signaled to put the body in the grave. But before they could even cover it over, the faint and then undeniable scent of roses sprang up.

None of them could look at the other, the orange sellers told us, for they knew better than they knew their own hearts that there were no roses here.

"Dios mío," was all they said. The mother got down on her knees in the dirt, and said all five decades of the rosary. The priest paced back and forth. The girl began to question her dead grandmother in Spanish and English and a singsong patois they had never heard.

But the man who had arranged it all, he was radiant. That man stepped back from the little band of mourners and deeply breathed in the scent of the roses. A strange calm came over him, they said, and in a voice as beautiful as song he told them all how much he loved this town.

3
A Cow in the Rain
1942

They were furious with each other that day, and with the rain. In that matter they were one. They had both felt it at the same time, the need to face what they only thought was the enemy, the rain. The rain had been with us for a week, a cold rain, cold and impertinent like all rain, and it marked the beginning of winter. It came on first as only a scent, then a feeling, then a sprinkle that blossomed into a steady downpour from a gray sky so low it seemed to press in on the world.

Now it was the endless stretch of time between the eleven o'clock High Mass and the relief of the evening meal.

No one was in the streets but them.

"This is what it will be like at the end of the world, Frederick," she said.

They walked about together in the town, past the square, around the back of the church, out by the old cemetery.

He began to speak. As he did only to alleviate the fits of ill humor brought on by the rain, he spoke longingly of his

youth, recalling pleasant times in the faraway house on Beacon Hill whose warm hearth and soft lamplight made it im-
pregnable to the very idea of cold and damp.

Ayela stared straight ahead, not listening. "How sad it is
to be the rain and be so despised," she said with a sigh. They
turned the corner in step.

He carried a black umbrella, she a green parasol pur-
chased from the Chinese in the market. Her skirt was soaked
from the knees down and on her face was a sullen expression. Goose bumps rose on her arms, for she had stubbornly
refused to wear a warm sweater under her raincoat.

The seeds of their first and enduring attraction grated
on them: her beauty, his wealth, her abrupt ways, his mortal
kindness, her terrible need, her high Mayan cheekbones, his
pipe tobacco, her occasional artistry, his sense of duty, his
long slender fingers, her unreasonableness, his coming to
this town on the edge of Mexico, her inability to leave it.

This infuriating paradox ran like a thread through their
marriage, and they had not been at it long enough to take a
deep breath and look out at the horizon when the incon-
gruity of their love capsized them. They did not know that
chafing against the shackles of marriage left scars of its own,
so that each fresh reminder of their differences exasperated
and set them at each other. The force of the rain drowned
out their shouting. They circled around the deserted town
for the better part of the afternoon, down Dolorosa Street,
Obispo Street, the lower town. Shouting at each other, then
hoping, blindly trying to strike some new and unimaginable
note that would let them go on together.

The rain came down in torrents, obliterating every-thing. Nothing was alive around them, no scent of anything but earth, which smelled vaguely of metal, of blood. No low, fecund hum of growth, the rain had totally obliterated that. No light, no shadows, just a sorrowful gray soup that was working itself into their bones, and a maddening chill. Rain soaked her hair, making a heavy sodden mass of it. Rain puddled on the cobblestones. They slogged along, indiffer-ent to their soaked feet.

In front of the courthouse they stopped to continue the argument. An old lover, the cook's recipe for chicken, an imagined slight, the brand of sugar they were using, the manners of the eldest boy: She accused, he denied. He ac-cused, she denied. Neither would give up the violence of having to be right.

"Go back where you came from!" came her last dare. The rain made her crazy, made her want to jump out of her skin. Couldn't he understand it, this craziness? "Go away, you bastard," she shouted at him.

"And where would you be if I did?" he challenged.

Had they forgotten that their children were growing nicely? That their house was fine? That the lemon balm grew in the courtyard and that no one pursued them? Had they forgotten they were blessed?

By the time they doubled back to the square, a cow had wandered in and stood like a mournful statue, at once de-feated by and quiescent in the rain. They stared at the eyes, heavy brown cow eyes that bore with dignity the burden of keeping the world awash in milk, silently suffering all the pulling, pulling, pulling on the hard, swollen teats day after endless day.

A profound pity rushed through them, first her, then him.

Frederick slapped the cow on the rump, hoping it would move on.

This compassion for the cow hit with such thrust and gravity that they had to laugh at themselves: what was the trouble? It was as though they had never heard of cows getting wet. Didn't they know what happened to animals in the rain? They looked around, but there was no one to turn to, or even appreciate their dilemma. He tried to make light of it, walk away, but she pulled on his sleeve, and spoke earnestly to him. He saw that, and played along.

She began to run in the direction of their house. He followed. When they opened the door, it was a foreign world that greeted them. The rooms were large and well furnished, the hearth fire suffused the house in warmth, the maid was humming in the kitchen, the children playing on the floor.

Ayela didn't call to them. In the face of that poor animal in the rain it seemed unimaginable to stop and embrace her children, even call them by name. She went to fetch blankets from the rooms upstairs.

"A rope," he said, tracking his wet boots through the rooms. "Where is a rope?"

The maid looked at them as if they were mad.

Husband and wife had the same thought: they would heap the blankets over the wet hide of the cow, dry it, put a rope around it, and lead it away from the square. Out toward the Olaca road? Back to the field it had wandered away from?

They ran all the way to the square. She trailed him, panting to keep up.

There was no letup in the rain and the town seemed darker, melting into itself, less real. To their dismay, the cow had wandered off and in its place was only the ravenous wet hunger of the day.

Clutching their blankets, they stood apart in the rain with a sense of failure. Their chests had ripped open to reveal their hearts, and having exposed their hearts to the air, they scarcely knew what to do with them.

Neither spoke.

Without the cow to defend, they were at a loss for a reason to go on together, and teetered dangerously at the precipice of mutual indifference. He might leave, she might run off, and the other would weep with relief. They were at that point in a falling-out that if reconciliation did not come, the rift between them would continue its silent and implacable advance, eventually setting them on opposite shores, two people who once knew each other.

As always, the first move was his.

He glanced at her, but she was looking the other way, probably in hopes of spotting the cow.

After a time, he spoke. "Don't worry. She's stronger than we are," he offered by way of détente.

His wife kept looking the other way in stubborn silence.

"Come on," he said. "You're soaked to the bone. You need a hot brandy."

With an injured look, she maintained her silence.

"For God's sake, Ayela, what is the point?" he asked, frustration mounting.

For a minute he thought she might scream at him, but she disappointed him, folding her arms across her chest and not deigning to glance in his direction.

"Not again," he said in disgust, already dreading the hours, perhaps days, of the icy silence, the guestroom bed, the maid's raised eyebrow, the children's bewilderment, the breakfast taken at his office, the dinners out, the watered-down coffee, his own foul temper.

"Ridiculous business," he muttered finally, and began to walk back toward the house.

As soon as he left, her body stiffened. Without turning around, she felt him departing in a dangerous kind of defeat, with the tail-down, wet-dog look of him walking away from her becoming the greatest misfortune she could imagine.

She closed her parasol and stood looking up into the pouring rain. Her voice was small and hesitant. It almost didn't come. She had to force it up through nearly impene-trable strata of pride and resentment, quickly, without turn-ing around and while he was still close enough to hear.

"You won't leave me, will you, Frederick?"

The words seemed stuck in the air, unable to find their destination. Through the rain they sounded as weightless and raw as a wrinkled newborn.

But they reached him like beautiful, distant music he had not heard before, and caused him to stop short and turn around. "Never," he said, rushing to fill the shimmering wet world of her face with kisses.

"Never."

4

The Pork Butcher and the Rich Man's Wife

1948

Half a lifetime after he had her on the floor of her mother's dress shop one stifling Saturday night, Gabriel Frank, the pork butcher, presented himself to the woman he had tried ever since to forget. After all that time without a word, he approached her in the town square on the day Eduardo Santos swung through on his electoral campaign, promising to make Santa Rosalia the crown jewel in the arc of the Rio Grande.

The meeting was anything but premeditated.

Gabriel Frank awoke that morning with a start from a dream that he was skimming the waves in a boat built of cork. He turned over, and instead of falling headlong into the beatific scent of the sea, he was greeted by the tortured breathing of his asthmatic wife. Groping through the murk of dawn, he rose and brewed his coffee, which he brooded over beside the stone fireplace, nursing a headache and the feeling that his dreams would always be better than his life.

Eventually, his wife appeared in the doorway. "I told you warm milk is good for insomnia," she said with a yawn.

"I've been taking it every night for a month," he replied.

His wife, who was twelve years older than Gabriel Frank and quite stout, studied him a moment and then changed the subject. "Your white shirt is ironed," she told him.

"What for?"

"For Eduardo Santos," she said. "Everyone will be there."

"Everyone but me," he grunted.

Throwing his coffee into the fireplace, he set out to grind pork butt for sausages in the butcher shop, which occupied the other half of the house. But by nine o'clock curiosity got the better of him, and he hung up his fat-stained apron and walked into town alone.

The day was bright and the heat had not yet begun in earnest.

He sat on a bench in front of the grocer's to watch people making preparations for the public rally in the square.

While her three sons chased each other in the sunlight, Ayela Linde was speaking to the man who was directing the workers setting up the podium at the top of the square. Gabriel Frank couldn't take his eyes off her. Rarely had he seen her since the day she had become a rich man's wife and forsook the place of her birth, moving up the hill to her new life and taking with her all that he had ever hoped for.

The longer he stared at her black hair and arrogant mouth and the curve of her bare arm in her blue summer dress, all the longing and rancor and rage of his entire life came rushing back and turned on her like a well-aimed arrow.

Samos the grocer came out of his shop and saw Gabriel Frank scowling. "What's the matter? Don't you like the smell of the shit we're selling today?" he asked jovially. Seeing Gabriel Frank had no intention of responding, the grocer followed his gaze to the woman at the other end of the plaza. "Ah, the Queen," he said. "Too rich for our blood."

"What, are you kidding? She knows where she had it good," Gabriel Frank said and stubbed his cigarette out on the ground.

"Well, then she must have come down with a bad case of amnesia," the grocer said, laughing. He shook his head and, still chuckling, gave Gabriel Frank a good-natured slap on the back. "Even if she hadn't forgotten you, she wouldn't remember you."

"So you say," Gabriel Frank replied and stared at the dusty ground.

People were beginning to pour into the square.

The grocer poked him. "Don't look now, but here comes the woman of your dreams."

Gabriel Frank lifted his eyes to see his wife huffing up the hill in her ridiculous red shoes. He shook his head and, with a feeling of dejection, got up and wandered away before she could spot him.

His mind was full of Ayela Linde, the Ayela Linde who had moved so indifferently through the dark sea of those long-ago summer nights, driving the men wild with her hard laugh and impenetrable black eyes and the fact that not one of them had ever known what the hell she was talking about. He had been one of them, the men who didn't know whether to have her or kill her or both, the men who she left howling like dogs because she hadn't even had the decency to hate them.

What was it she used to say? Something about ever since birth when her mama's milk refused to flow, she knew that the world held nothing she needed. Or anyone else needed, for that matter. What the hell kind of talk was that?

A crowd had formed around the podium at the head of the square. Gabriel Frank elbowed his way through, coming up behind Ayela Linde, so close he could smell on her the same flowery vanilla perfume that had nearly knocked him off his feet fourteen years ago.

Her hair was pulled up on top of her head, and before him was the luxury of her bare shoulders. He burned his gaze into them in hopes that his intensity of feeling would scald her or at least make her turn toward him with a little hum of recognition.

Lighting a cigarette, he vowed to himself that she would hear his new voice, the voice of his better self, speaking to her of nothing as if it were something, as if he had knowledge as profound and unsettling as her own.

At a little before ten, the carnival wagons rolled in along Dolorosa Street, followed by a windowless truck with a megaphone on its roof shouting unintelligible promises in English and Spanish. The boatlike automobile of Eduardo Santos followed. Women ran into the square with roast turkeys and bowls of oranges. People brought the sick to stand in the shade of the sabal palms along the edge, as though Eduardo Santos were the Supreme Pontiff and not a politician churning out the senescent promises of an electoral campaign.

A moment later Eduardo Santos himself, followed by his aides, stepped out of the car and climbed the steps to the podium. His white suit was a tight fit on a body that was too fond of food and already soaked in sweat. He had thin black hair and a thin moustache that he could not stop touching.

Eduardo Santos stood silent at the podium, scanning the sky. When he was sure of the crowd's attention, he brightened as if inspiration had just struck and launched into the same speech he had made half an hour before in the parched town of Oderada.

His very person hit the people like a revelation. They saw not so much what they would become as what they could become in the glossy eyes of the man who promised the bug zappers and trees with grapefruits the color of rubies and the railroad spur that would cause prosperity to break over Santa Rosalia in a gentle and unending wave.

The moment those golden words were uttered by Eduardo Santos, his assistants applauded, beating spoons on old kitchen pots.

Eduardo Santos silenced them with a look. His expression darkened, and he mopped his face with a silk handkerchief. "Though it will come, that day is a far-off day," he said glumly into the microphone. "In the meanwhile, we have our problems, don't we, my friends?"

His gaze fell on a man in the first row. He asked the man his name.

"George Hildar," the man said.

"Alright, George Hildar. What is your biggest problem in life?"

George Hildar thought. "Money," he said. "I need a wife who spits out money, not swallows it up."

The crowd laughed.

Eduardo Santos laughed harder.

Then he signaled to his aides. "Well, George," he said. "I can't give you a money machine. But I can give you a chicken."

An aide brought out a squawking chicken under his arm and placed it flailing and pecking the air in the hands of George Hildar.

The people laughed and cheered.

Eduardo Santos scanned the crowd for another victim.

Gabriel Frank was laughing so hard at the chicken trying to escape from George Hildar that for a moment he forgot about Ayela Linde.

But only for a moment. Out of the corner of his eye he caught her patting her nose with a pink pad and reddening her lips. As she held up the little compact mirror, admiring her made-up face and the swan's neck that rose from her starched summer dress, Gabriel Frank felt shabby. He looked down at his fingernails, which were dirty with pork fat, and lamented that he had not bothered to wash his hands or wear the shirt his wife had ironed.

Ayela Linde took a pale blue fan from her purse and moved off into the crowd, calling to her youngest boy not to stray too far. It was the first time Gabriel Frank had heard her voice in years and it was a mother's voice, sweeter than he remembered, like ripe melon.

The butcher followed her through the crowd. He stopped when she stopped, and stood behind her.

Eduardo Santos was giving a corn plant to an old woman with a gold tooth.

Gabriel Frank stubbed out his cigarette and lit another. Now she's going to see who I am, he promised himself. "He's a card," he spoke at the left ear of Ayela Linde.

"Yes," she said automatically without facing him.

He leaned farther, toward her, and said in an even voice, "It's the same story as always. It's been the same story for a thousand years."

She turned his way and stared at him for a full moment as if trying to place him.

Gabriel Frank felt his heart go to the moon. He fumbled for something else to say. All he could manage was to repeat, "Always the same thing."

She glanced at him again and then turned her attention to the show Eduardo Santos was putting on. He had come down from the podium and was shaking the hands of the schoolchildren that were going to sing for him.

"You can never have what you want, what you want flies right out of your hand like a bird," he continued, beginning to feel lost in the thick soup of his words.

She turned toward him. "Yes," she said, her ostrich eyes sweeping over him.

The pork butcher ransacked his mind for some response that would keep those eyes on him. He felt it coming, right there, ready to be spoken, and opened his mouth to let fate play its hand. But she was moving on through the crowd, slipping through the ranks of schoolchildren standing at attention, ready to begin their song.

Gabriel Frank couldn't believe it when Ayela Linde stepped out in front of the children and stood face-to-face with Eduardo Santos.

It happened so quickly that, if he had looked away, it would have been over.

Ayela Linde rapped Eduardo Santos across the cheek with her blue fan.

Eduardo Santos looked startled.

The butcher didn't understand. He heard her say to Eduardo Santos, "Shame on you. You're the enemy of us all, giving us what we have no use for," and he saw Eduardo Santos rub his cheek where it had been struck. Then the men in sand-colored uniforms came and grabbed Ayela Linde by the arm and led her away.

Eduardo Santos stopped long enough to watch her disappear around the corner. Then he went on with the show.

Gabriel Frank stood gaping like an idiot.

Letting out a sigh of defeat for Eduardo Santos and for himself and with a conviction that frightened him, he began to sink into the quicksand of the emptiness and confusion that overwhelmed him that night in her mother's shop when Ayela Linde got up from the floor and dressed and stepped around him as though he were just another bug crawling in a world she despised. All that disgust, for what? He had never been able to understand her dissatisfaction, because he himself was having the time of his life.

Having lost his reason to be present, Gabriel Frank drifted away from the crowd. He stopped at the opposite end of the square, where three children were taking turns jumping off a bench.

Gabriel Frank approached the eldest, a serious boy of about nine. "I am an old friend of your mama," he said in a gentle voice.

"Hello, then," said the boy. "Can you tell us what just happened?"

Gabriel Frank lit a cigarette. "No, I can't."

Seeing his brother talking to a grown-up, the smallest boy ran up. He couldn't have been more than three or four years old and, unlike his brothers, bore a strong resemblance to his mother. "I want my mama," he said. "I'm hungry."

"Come with me, then," said Gabriel Frank. He walked to the edge of the square and turned around. Right behind him stood the three boys with expectation in their eyes.

Then it came to him.

He will never have Ayela Linde. Ever. She is too far beyond him, like spider silk floating in space, always out of reach. She will never look at him, eyes large with expectation.

But here are her children.

They are ready to listen to him.

They want him.

And he will take them.

While their mother is busy explaining herself to their father and the mayor and Eduardo Santos, he will take the children. Take them home with him. Send his wife into the house and close up the butcher shop and pull down the shades and put a white cloth on the table in the shop kitchen. He will select the best chops, the center cut.

While the chops are cooking, he will speak to the boys of the way things should be: bright, simple, beautiful. He will speak about the day his own father gave him his first pork butcher tools. He will tell them of his happiness on that day when his life was revealed to him and the universe took on a blessed order. He will tell them how he saw truth open up before him as clear and uncomplicated as the morning light, the truth that surely shines with the same glow for every living being.

The boys might not understand. They might smirk and look away.

Then, he will be forced to take the old case lined with black velvet down from the top shelf and open it for them. At first they will shrink back, frightened, but in time they will come to marvel at the double-edged cleaver, the twelve-inch pig splitter, the skinning knife, the bow saw, knowing, without being told, that there is nothing that does not yield to them.

Yes, he will speak about his views to the three boys of Ayela Linde.

He will speak to them wisely and without remorse.

They will understand. They will not look right through him as though he were nothing more than air. They will not regard him as a joke. They will not humiliate him.

They will behold him with dark serious eyes, ravenous for what he will say next.

Yes, he will go slowly.

He will speak to them for as long as it takes.

This time, with these children, he will not fail.

This will be something that he can understand. That everyone can understand.

Gabriel Frank felt a sudden urge to run. "Come on," he called to the children. "Hurry up before we all go to the dogs."

5
Where God Put Us
1951

They've always had trouble with that one, and I've taken care of them all. Mr. Xavier, the first, he was the worst crier, a sweet boy, but crying from day one, always finding something to be sad about, happy that the first day of summer has come, but sad that the first day of summer means the last day of spring. Then Mr. Freddie, chubby and bald like an old man, and fussy, too fussy to be sad, and then the youngest, Jesse, never a tear, smiling and cooing from the minute he got up. Fearless from the moment he was born, always reaching too far, for the highest branches, the deepest water, running away at every chance.

Now he's seven, nearly eight, and he jumps from everything, trying to fly like a bird. It's no surprise to me.

The señora laughs. "Flying," she says. "Why not?"

The Monsignor threw him out of school. "Insolence. We won't have it here," he told her.

That made the señora laugh harder. "The Monsignor! I

knew him when his knees shook because the old ladies looked at him the wrong way."

"Yes, señora." There is nothing for me to do but pour her morning coffee. But then I had to say, "We should stay where God put us."

The señora never listens to me. "Concha," she said, "if I had stayed where I was put, I'd be dead by now. And sometimes I think I didn't get far enough away."

The señora's mother, Felidia Garzón, walked into the kitchen scowling as usual, her black hair streaked with white pulled back in a small bun. She sat down at the table and glared at her grandson. "Don't you go to school?"

"I'm expelled," Jesse said proudly.

Felidia Garzón scowled harder. "That boy will be the ruin of you," she said to her daughter. She shook a finger at Jesse — "Flying, indeed!" — and turned again to the señora. "And what does Frederick say? No. You don't have to tell me. He's left it to you. Men. Useless creatures!" She smoothed a stray hair, and started in again: "You should have had girls. What am I going to do with all those dresses?" Felidia Garzón went on, talking about her dress shop where she was happy, before the arthritis in her hands set in, before she grew heavy and old and began dragging herself from doctor to doctor. It was a jewel box of a shop, painted soft pink and smelling of lavender. The dresses hung on satin hangers, red, coral, sea green dresses.

Felidia Garzón sighed. "Do you remember that peach satin with the stand-up collar? And that green with the beaded top?" Her voice ran down and was silent a minute, but before she could grow sad she turned her attention to Jesse again. "You let him run wild!" she said, glowering at her grandson.

"What do you know about children?" the señora said.

"I had you, didn't I?"

The señora didn't answer.

This is what people said: One day long ago a traveling judge came to Santa Rosalia to hear the trial of a man who stole from the poor box. The judge had a stern look, and he came off the bench and put his face up to old Nebo's, asking, "Are you poor?" Nebo shook his head yes. "Then the money belongs to you," said the judge. "Just pass some of it around to your friends." After he let Nebo off, the judge came by Felidia Garzón's looking for a bauble to take back to his wife. He liked what he saw, the dresses and the dressmaker, and Felidia Garzón closed the shop early and drew the shades and the judge walked out whistling the next morning and was never heard from again. Felidia Garzón didn't miss a day of work, the midwife came to the shop to deliver the baby and the next day a cradle appeared, and Felidia Garzón sewed more furiously than ever. All the dresses for a long while after were red, red as the blood she lost with the baby. The child grew up, learning about the world from the pretty girls who blew up from Mexico with the breeze and were hired by Felidia Garzón to cut patterns. Then her hands began to stiffen and ache, and she hurled the first electric sewing machine Santa Rosalia ever had in the trash bin, and went to sit in the square, hardening her heart against the world.

The señora had had enough. She stood up and took her coffee cup over to the sink. "Look at the time, Mother. Let's go," she said. "Which doctor is it today?"

I was quartering three chickens for dinner and he scared me to death.

"Hola, Concha."

"Get down off that icebox!" I yelled at him.

"Okay, I'll fly down."

"No. You cannot fly."

"Yes, I can."

"Where do you want to go anyway?"

"Around up in the sky."

"What's there? There is nothing up there."

"There are clouds, I can eat the clouds."

"I'll bake you a meringue instead."

"No, I want to fly through the clouds."

"Why do you want to leave us?"

"It's not that."

"Jesse! Get down here, bad boy, or I'll put you in the soup."

He landed so close to me he almost knocked me down.

He is maddening, like his mother. Not at all like his father. What a grand man his father is, so handsome in his white linen suit, and so kind. In the morning before he leaves for the courthouse, coming to the kitchen: "Concha, what will it be tonight? Oxtail stew? Fritters in almond sauce?" And he puts the fingers of his right hand together and kisses them. "You are spoiling me!"

That Jesse, I could shake him. "Go and do your school-work now," I told him.

He ran right out of the house. I saw him running toward the field.

I told the señora when she returned from the doctor's.

"He's a boy who likes to go," she said.

"He is a boy who does not know where to stop," I said.

The señora laughed. "That's just the way he is. You worry too much, Concha."

I asked her, "How much is too much?"

Then I surprised even myself. I told the señora about me, about when I was a young girl in my country. I spent my days sitting on the broken step outside the deserted train station. The sun beat down on my head and I counted the weeds growing up through the tracks, waiting, dreaming of the train. The train never stopped in my village, but one day it did, a man got on, a man with a straw hat and cardboard suitcase, all he did was climb the iron stairs and the door closed and a long grunt came from the train and slowly it started down the tracks, then sped away as fast as it could so that not a trace of it remained. Not even its memory. So easy.

One day I put my two dresses and my lucky mustard seed charm in a straw bag and went to the station and waited in the broiling sun for the train and it came and I got on. A man in a blue uniform asked for my ticket. I had none, but something in me said, "On the other end, they'll have the money for my ticket." He was a nice man, he must have had a girl like me because he said, "Are you sure? Alright, we won't say anything about it until Cali."

I forgot about the money and the man. Out the window, the banana plantations and the worn-out hills flew past, and after the train pulled out of a town called Pula, where the station peddlers sold meat pies, I felt hungry. In my bag was a cake and a bun and a banana, I ate them all at once, that was all the food I brought. I talked to no one and kept my eyes straight ahead, breathing quickly because I was thrilled to be free and on the train and rushing away so fast that no one could say where I was. But after a while the heat got to me, my thoughts died and my eyes closed, I must have slept a long time because when I woke the train was stopped in a big dark depot. The men stood over me, the conductor with the nice face, and the others. "Okay, where's the money for your ticket?" they asked. "We're in Cali." Their faces were ugly, just like their voices, which got louder and louder.

There I was, a girl of fourteen sitting in a dark empty train with not enough money for the ticket and no one who knew her. What do you think that girl had to do?

The señora stood up slowly. "Oh, Concha," she said and put her hand on my cheek, and in a walk that was wobbly as though she had drunk too much anisette, she went out of the room, feeling sorry for my suffering.

I saw that I hadn't made myself clear.

In the mornings, the señora went here and there, and in the afternoons around to Rosalba Vilar's for a lemonade and a chat on the patio where a parrot named Rafael could say the names of constellations in three languages.

Jesse stayed with me.

Right by my side I kept him at Cassava's Market and at Hosta's where I got new oxford cloth shirts for the boys, right alongside me while I cut the white roses which we wrapped in wet paper and carried in our arms to Sister Alphonzina de las Cruces for the altar.

But the minute I turned my back, he was out on the roof.

He stood looking at the sky.

Then he began to walk, holding his arms out, like he was on a tightrope.

When he saw my frightened face, he said, "Don't worry, Concha. I know I can fly." How sweetly he said it, not at all like a naughty boy. But like a boy who knows.

"Now crawl back in the window the way you got out!" I scolded him, even though it was useless.

I should have seen it before. It was already there, had always been there, in his little boy's body, in the restless eyes, in the voice. In everything about him. Not today or tomorrow, but someday, somehow or other, he will go from us with the grace and indifference of a bird.

I went right to the señora. She was sitting at the table, doing the household accounts. "Some children make it hard for themselves," I said and sat down with her like one of the family and out came the other part of my story. The part that I could choke to death and cut to bits and throw to the bottom of the sea it was so horrible. My voice was flat and I looked at my hands on the table. I told the señora all about my mama, whose own milk fed me, and my papa, who walked with me whistling along the riverbank, and my little brothers and sisters, Eduardo and Diego and Chula and Ursula, who came running to me and clung to me with all the strength of their little child arms when dreams of three-headed monsters woke them in the night. My own family. My own family that I left without a word on a Thursday afternoon twenty-three years ago. My own family, as beautiful and as fleeting as the señora's white cabbage roses in the center of the table. And now they've moved on, where I don't know.

Neither of us spoke. We were lost in a strange quiet.

All the while I was praying: Don't be so stubborn, señora. Don't make us all suffer. Listen to what life is telling you through the words of a poor housemaid.

Then suddenly she jumped up like she remembered everything. She ran out of the house, screaming for Jesse.

He was only playing in the dirt by the garden.

"Get inside," she said in a low voice. "I want to talk to you."

She had a murderous look on her face.

For that, I thanked God.

6
Scenes from the World
1955

Of course I had seen her picture in the local papers, at this event and that, looking wealthy and grand, as much as one can in these small towns of ours. So seeing her in person was a bit of a shock. She must have been in her late thirties at the time, but she looked no more than a girl, tall and trim, with her long hair loose. She was still a beautiful creature, though there was nothing like that between us. Not that I wouldn't have liked it, but she seemed above that sort of thing, married as she was and presumably happily, and not interested in her own beauty, just in the task at hand.

She walked in and sat down in the chair in front of my desk and looked at me as if she had a terrible burden to unload. She never said as much, but it was in her every movement.

"My husband has given me an assignment," she said slowly. "To make arrangements for a trip to celebrate our twentieth wedding anniversary." She shifted her weight in the chair. "Anywhere in the world."

Not the usual request, I have to say. I'm lucky if I sold a trip to Monterrey or the Port of Morado or up to the Big City, as people here referred to Laredo. I myself am a great traveler, and had just taken this position to build up a little cash to finance my next trip, a sojourn to investigate the splendid desolation of the Patagonian plains. Always on the move, I am. I'm a collector of it all, you see.

What I mean by "it all" are those simple and often mysterious scenes, those slivers of inexpressible beauty that one finds in far-off places and that, quite frankly, I am starved for in this insipid part of the world. What scenes am I talking about? Not the great sights. On the contrary, the smallest of images caught from the corner of the eye, gloriously unfamiliar, yet striking some deeply familiar chord. The tea pickers swarming the green hills of Ceylon, for example. Berbers leading their camels through the ripples of cinnamon sands. The sober expression of the young groom in Punjab. The women arguing over the price of oranges in the marketplace in Port-of-Spain. The blind girl in a red coat, staring at the blue Mediterranean with eyes transfigured by ecstasy.

Yes, I can get carried away, can't I?

Now then, Mrs. Linde. I found her not at all superior, but deferential and even a bit timid, but that may be because she was out of her element, I knew about the world, and she by her own admission had never been more than a hundred miles from the town of her birth.

Her husband had suggested Paris for their anniversary trip. She repeated the name of the city. "So fragile. It sounds like the rustling of old paper." She said it in such a noncommittal tone that I didn't know whether or not she liked the idea. Nevertheless, I launched into a description of the Opéra and the Bois de Boulogne and the others that were de rigueur with visitors, speaking in a phony French accent that I had picked up in a summer of grape picking in Alsace. And of course the Loire, and I pulled out the brochure of those glorious châteaux, Chenonceau, of course, and the extravagant Chambord, which she folded and put in her pocketbook and sat there gazing into space.

What woman would refuse such a trip? Well, maybe it was the husband she was refusing, it occurred to me, but then again, no, it didn't seem so. Women are no good at hiding hatred for their men, and from her came no sneers, no complaints, not the least little innuendo or grimace as regarded him.

Since I couldn't fathom what might be running through her mind, I contented myself with her face. The nose was classically long and straight, a portraitist's dream, the brows thick but well-shaped. Never had I seen such skin without a mark, and that wide expanse of lineless cheek with the slightest tinge of café au lait, like a heroine in a old Spanish novel.

Well, by that time Mrs. Linde had had enough of gazing into nothingness and rose without warning. "Thank you," she said. "You are very thorough." And with that she was gone, back in the blue Buick to her everyday life.

Too bad.

To my surprise, she returned the middle of the following week. But her first visit had set the precedent for all others. Her interest was polite, if vague, as though I were showing her patterns for slipcovers she didn't really need.

Not once when she came to see me did I delve into the logistics of a trip, the procuring of passports and visas and changing of planes and trains, for fear of losing her entirely.

She said very little at our meetings, and the less she said, the more I wanted to sell her a trip, not for the money, but because I wanted her to need something from me. When you are ready with the world and it is rebuffed, it is maddening.

She was not a creature of habit, but would arrive at any time of day when the children were in school, driving the blue behemoth of a Buick. It crossed my mind that her indifference to traveling might stem from a reluctance to leave the children. But really, she never spoke of them or showed their pictures or looked at her watch nervously so as to leave on time to pick them up, so to me it was apparent they were not uppermost in her mind. Her reluctance came from something else, not fear, because her indifference was real and not a smokescreen for some deeper emotion.

Though she didn't give a reason, I could understand that Paris was not for her, too standard, too talked about, too easily disappointing, and I forgave, even admired her for that. On the second visit I suggested Buenos Aires, Córdoba, a trip up to Machu Picchu. She had some Latin in her, anyone could see that, and I thought it might appeal. Yet one must approach delicately in these situations, one can't come right out and say: Go back to where you came from. Her interest was piqued at the mention of Cartagena, and she looked intently at the travel photos of the old walled city. "Is it as beautiful as they say?" she wanted to know. And I could

see her there, walking the streets of balconied viceregal res-
idences, descending through the old slave quarters, past the
fetid marshes to the Caribbean beaches and the nefarious
port which had once been a smugglers' paradise of emeralds
and precious metals, Paramaribo parrots and Amazon monkeys, dark rum and African slaves, giving each world its
due consideration. But she folded up the travel pamphlet
neatly, creasing the folds precisely the right way. Did I
imagine a sere disappointment in her voice when she put it
in her bag, saying, "My husband and I will discuss it"?

Just as I thought, she came back the next week ready to
try again. Maybe the old man had put the kibosh on the
Latin journey. Though, on the other hand, it wouldn't have
surprised me if she had never even shown him the travel
brochures. She was secretive, that was obvious, and who
knows what kinds of things she was capable of hiding?

I must admit, I was becoming a bit exasperated with her
lack of enthusiasm. I would have given my eyeteeth to be in
her shoes. Even to be dragged to Paris with all the other
sheep, there is always something to be gained, if only to
breathe in the air of a new place.

Still, my pulse quickened when the Buick pulled up outside the travel agency and she got out and put the dime in
the parking meter and walked toward our door. Of course,
she had no idea that she kept me going, kept me from falling
off the cliff into the slough of dull-as-dustness. She graced
our charmless white-walled office in her multihued outfits,
such an unusual mixing of colors, the violet and the yellow,
the red and pale blue, not at all like the pastel shirtwaists

that women wore in those days. A sense of color and style that suggested an artistic nature and led me to ask her if she painted. How uncomplicated she was. She smiled and shook her head no, "Not unless you mean the kitchen walls."

Suspecting rejection of the Latin American plan, for the third visit I had prepared a package for her on an African safari. But she did not warm to the idea of camping, albeit royally, in the bush. I detected that at once by the tiniest sustained blink of the eyes, and the slightly longer than usual exhale when I spoke of the intense darkness of African night and the desolate cries of the wild beasts. Well then, what about Scandinavia, I suggested, New York, the Costa del Sol, Marrakech, the Aegean, and I launched into a lecture on the Levant, with obscure and erudite references which shamed me the minute they flew over her head.

She left with armfuls of brochures that were returned unopened the following week. Good God, woman, I wanted to shout, what is it you want?

My impatience didn't betray me, I'm proud to say, and I let the brochures lie where she put them on my desk. Leaning back in my chair and resting the back of my head against my palms, I closed my eyes and spoke to her of Central Asia, where I had recently spent eight months traveling from ancient city to ancient city in search of the beginning of time. There were no brochures for that. Perhaps that's what she wanted, some uncertainty, some magic. I spoke of Tashkent on the Silk Road and Samarqand, Tamerlane's beloved capital, both with their golden light and mausoleums and names of foods she had never heard. I described the scenes one might stumble on, the surprising tableaux, labyrinthine streets, the big-eyed children dashing among the warren of stalls in the bazaars, the pomegranate trees, the cotton harvest, the thick-bearded men in capes and knee-length boots, the cupolas dripping with gold. The strange music and ritualistic, often frantic and, yes, frightening dancing at certain festivals, and in a melodramatic lowering of my voice, the questionable ceremonies that unfortunately still take place in the window-less salons off the narrow alleys. She seemed to relax in her chair and remain attentive, even to like listening to me, and for that I was enormously grateful, with these provincial people here I don't have the chance to go on about such things. She didn't stop me in any event, and left with such an air of lively curiosity I thought I might have cracked the case of the travel preferences of Mrs. Linde.

However, after that meeting she did not return. She never booked a trip through me, and I admit that over the following months, I inquired of my counterparts in the neighboring towns, and not one of them had been visited by a Mr. or Mrs. Linde.

Well, I couldn't seem to let the matter of Mrs. Linde go. That little preoccupation cost me my job. Before long I found myself fired from the travel agency for "a poor atti-tude" and no sales. What a funk I was in. There was no go-ing to faraway places in that kind of humor and with the few pennies I had to my name anyhow, so I did what I did. The week of her anniversary, I drove down to Santa Rosalia and spotted her walking her children to school, going on in that languid way that people do when there is nothing out of the ordinary coming up in their lives.

Such a pity.

Shameful as it was, I sank even lower. Some discreet inquiries turned up the information I needed, and on the night of her wedding anniversary, I drove down again to Santa Rosalia and parked just down the street from the Linde house, like a criminal casing the place. As soon as the car came to a standstill, I began to berate myself: What if they're having a party *en famille,* or have already left, or, worse yet, are merely staying in?

But she did not disappoint. A little before eight o'clock, they came out of the house, both of them dressed in white, looking resplendent and cool. He was a pleasant enough looking chap, all Anglo, taller than she and with an affable air that said he'd as soon be anywhere to celebrate their anniversary as long as he was with her and she with him.

They did not drive their car, but walked down to the town, a matter of a few blocks, and to my great surprise went into the pool hall, a place frequented by lowlifes and refugees from across the border.

I followed a distance behind so as not to be seen. There was an open-air dance floor at the back of the pool hall, and they went right over and began to dance to the small band that was playing a soppy Mexican ranchera. I sat across the room at the bar in order to view their every move.

A loud, cheap, smoky place that smelled of stale beer. So this was what Mrs. Linde had turned down the world for. I nodded to the bartender to bring me another drink.

The booze took the edge off my aggravation, and before long the outdoor dance floor seemed attractive, and the band had switched to a livelier tempo, which wasn't as offensive. Mr. and Mrs. Linde were good dancers, they knew how to get out of each other's way, and there was a manner they had of looking at each other, as if the whole thing were too hilarious but it would be impolite to break out laughing. At one point people cleared a circle around them to dance, clapping while they spun and twirled and dipped.

Around one o'clock a fight broke out in the bar, and they left.

I hung back watching them walk up into the square, which was deserted and, in the moonlight, not unappealing.

There was nothing open around the square, even the hotel had fallen asleep, so I sat on the curb. In the center of the square Ayela Linde and her husband began to sing. They locked arms and were warbling out strains from *The Pirates of Penzance* like they were having the time of their lives. Mrs. Linde pointed at the sky. I couldn't quite hear her, but I think she said, "Look, they're falling!" and both of them gazed up with the rapture of children at the shower of stars shoot shoot shooting across the sky.

As I watched the grande dame of Santa Rosalia in her bare shoulders and flowing white skirts and her princely husband watching the stars my spirits began to lighten. I leaned back on my elbows to let what was taking place across the street wash over me and sink into the part of me that is immune to logic. The little scene began to burn itself into my mind, to take its place in memory alongside my other treasures.

How she spotted me I'll never know, but she began to wave excitedly in my direction. "Mr. Barber, come join us," she called out as though it were the most natural thing in the world. "Come join us."

Imagine that. Calling to me as if I was a longtime friend whom she was tickled to see. So genuine was her invitation, touched with an almost heartbreaking innocence, and it seemed to come right from the truth of who she was. It didn't even occur to her to ask why I was lying about the curb at two o'clock in the morning, or how to explain me to her husband, or inquire about my life and times at the travel agency. Omissions dearer to me than I can say.

Alright, it wasn't the apricot harvest in Pakistan or the tireless rickshaw driver in Varanasi, or the Parisian girl with painted eyes and black beret sitting alone in a crowded café.

My little scene in the square was none of those.

But it was something.

It was something alright.

And I was part of it.

7
The Grand Opening
1957

i

On the afternoon of June 10, a cloud of anticipatory excitement for the evening's event burst over Santa Rosalia, swirling through the town and the streets and the houses and reaching its inhabitants as exhilaration, agitation, anxiety, and, in a few cases, pure trepidation.

At the Linde household, chaos reigned.

The younger boys ran in and out of the house whooping and hollering louder than usual. Concha shouted at them to stop. "Quiet," their mother demanded of them all. "Your father is getting ready to go."

As Frederick Linde, dressed in khaki pants and a summer shirt, took his tuxedo from the hall closet, the family rushed at him.

"Why can't we come tonight?" Jesse wailed.

"Where will I meet you later?" Ayela Linde questioned her husband for the fourth time.

Concha asked again, "Will you be having dinner here tonight, Mr. Frederick?"

"Father, can I borrow a tie?" Xavier wanted to know.

Ayela Linde grabbed her husband's arm. "Frederick, where did you put that scroll I'm supposed to give the mayor?"

Their attention intensified the strange feeling of claustrophobia that had recently descended upon Frederick Linde. He took a deep breath, and with blistering patience ministered to their needs.

The family was oblivious to his pained efforts, and once its concerns were addressed, retreated in a wave to its own business, leaving Frederick Linde to take his departure more or less ignored, which irritated the man who had conceived and brought to life the idea of the Arts Pavilion that was to open that evening in a gala ceremony, bringing culture in the form of a music hall, an art gallery, a small theater, and rooms for art and dance lessons to the ham-fisted town of Santa Rosalia. The town had been slow to warm to an Arts Pavilion, but now that the cockamamie idea was about to become a reality, Santa Rosalia had stood up a little straighter, squared its shoulders, and puffed itself up with pride, as if it had arrived somewhere very desirable.

"Good-bye, then," Frederick called to no one in particular. He proceeded down the walk, tuxedo slung over his shoulder, to the silver Chrysler parked under the trees in front of the house. He got in and sat for a moment, enjoying the silence and the ticking of the idle engine.

Without thinking too much about it, he drove down

Olivea Road, took a right past the square, and headed out toward the Olaca road. He let the soothing motion of the car override the tangle of thoughts that ambushed him, driving down the old two-lane highway west, past the miles of citrus groves out to where the countryside opened up to stands of mesquite and dry stretches of no-man's-land.

Frederick Linde had no destination in mind.

Though he wasn't a drinking man, especially in the middle of the afternoon, on an impulse he pulled over at a roadside bar. Passing through the swinging door into the dark coolness, which smelled of cheap stale beer and sawdust, Frederick Linde felt himself having crossed over into a haven from himself. There were only two other patrons in the place, both of whom had probably been there since morning. Frederick took a stool at the back of the bar, satisfied that no acquaintance would find him here. From across the bar, where he was wiping the counter with a dry rag, the bartender, a hawk of a man with an acerbic air and powerful shoulders, took his order.

In slow sips Frederick drank his beer and indulged in his infrequent vice of smoking an unfiltered cigarette. Away from the certainty of his life, he settled in to what was on his mind. At forty-seven, Frederick Linde felt age dogging him, felt the regrets of having gone down the wrong path, felt that after all this time, he was no more than a slave to nothing he really cared about. Yet how was this possible when in his mind's eye he had just fled his Boston upbringing and, heading south with the ideals of a young man, had been stopped in his tracks by a woman in the unlikely town of Santa Rosalia?

His strongest image from those days was the stifling Saturday nights in the small rooms he took over the square where his beloved came to him, spilling her yards of hair onto his shoulders and backing him onto the bed where she made him the happiest man alive, and then vowing that she would not allow him to accompany her to church the following morning, because to watch someone get on their knees and pray is the most intimate act of all. He recalled that dictum of hers with fond amusement, still bewitched and proud of the eccentricities of the woman he married. On those Saturday nights when it was too hot to move, they had lain wrapped in each other's arms on that small rickety bed until it became too much for Ayela Garzón. She would get up and walk to the window where she stood naked, looking down at the square. The low lamplight lit her glorious form from behind and put him, his lust having been temporarily spent, in a state of high admiration, as though he were lost in one of those aimless afternoons among the classical statues in the Museum of Fine Arts.

From those evenings of pleasure had sprung his life.

But now, suddenly, it had become a life that pinned him down mercilessly under a web that was so dark and close he could barely see the light of day. Any attempt to wriggle free would surely be suicide. He felt a tightening in the chest at the lines that lashed him to a dozen creatures that needed him, depended on him, couldn't go on without his presence, sucked the life from him.

Frederick Linde stubbed out his cigarette.

It seemed that this mind-numbing servitude had come about blindingly fast, not, as was actually the case, as a result of the weeks and months and years of his own perfectly conscious decisions that had gotten him to where he was now, rational judgments that had come one after the other, day after day, welcomed and savored at the time.

He cursed at the futility of his situation, muttering, "Damn it to hell," under his breath and putting down his beer glass a little too hard.

The attention of the bartender was aroused. "Easy, pal," he called over from down the bar, looking at Frederick Linde to see if he had the smell of trouble about him.

"Sorry," Frederick replied.

The bartender looked at him coldly, but finally decided in Frederick's favor. "Another one?"

Frederick nodded.

The bartender brought over the beer. His voice maintained a kind of disinterested mockery. "What is it? Love troubles?" he said to Frederick with a pointed look and a sly smile.

Frederick laughed nervously. "Nothing like that."

"I see," the bartender said.

"Well, not exactly," Frederick said, slightly surprised by the possibility of unburdening himself to another human being.

"Do tell," the bartender said, maintaining his aloofness, but practicing the ancient and sacred purpose of his line of work, which had little to do with pouring drinks.

Frederick hesitated, feeling put on the spot. "There was an article in the paper last week. Thursday. On the back page of the front section. A wire story. Don't suppose you saw it," he went on, now with a desire to spill the whole damn thing even if it was only to fall on the cynical ears of the bartender.

The bartender shrugged his shoulders.

"Silly, I know," Frederick admitted. "But, you see, there was this mine in Brazil. Itabira." Even the name of the town had caught him off guard. Itabira. For some reason, it spoke persuasively to him. He could see himself there, in Itabira, which he imagined as a small village lodged at the foot of looming mountains, surrounded by the lousy, crumbling soil, and himself carrying buckets of dirt or hoisting unwieldy cuts of lumber onto his shoulder, or engaged in some other backbreaking, soul-saving work

"Itabira, one of the largest iron ore mines in the world," Frederick continued. "Worked by hand by locals. Two hundred fifty thousand tons every year. By hand. Can you imagine? And then put on some run-down trains to get it to port. None of them making more than a dime a week," he added with a glum empathy.

During the entire time, the bartender had been moving about behind the counter, dusting bottles, changing the position of glasses. "Tough luck," the bartender agreed. He took a toothpick from the shot glass on the counter and began to work his molars.

Frederick's voice took on an inspired tone, and he pressed on, aware of his own foolishness, yet unable to turn back. "But the thing about it is, some engineers, hired, of course, but still. They went down there, to Itabira, and rebuilt the railroad and the town and the mine. And the harbor. The whole thing. Damn rough going too. Had to bore through a mountain to get the water supply from the next town. And the mudslides during the rainy season." Frederick stopped for a moment to put a brake on the emotion welling up inside him. "Donkeys had to be pulled out. Men sunk in up to their waist. And most of the workers were poor locals who had never even thought about a tunnel. Still, they did it. Now they've got a new railroad and new locomotives to take the ore to the harbor. New machinery to work the mines. New harbor for the steamers to take the ore to Europe. New town to live in."

The bartender removed the toothpick from his mouth and considered Frederick Linde attentively. "So what's the problem?"

Frederick Linde hesitated. "No problem, really. It's just . . . Oh it's nothing." He took a swig of beer and started again. "It's just that . . . I'd have given my eyeteeth to be part of a thing like that." He said it sheepishly, as if he was a child spilling his greatest secret, understanding that since boyhood he had longed to be immersed in something large, something important, enjoying the camaraderie of workers who grumbled and complained yet every day came back to the grand scheme that would bring prosperity and hope to their country. Making the lot of countless people a little better, a little more tolerable, helping them secure a little patch of peace that only money could buy.

The bartender let out a low whistle. "So go find another rat's nest to straighten out. The world is full of them."

Frederick sighed. "Yes, but, there's . . . well, what I do now."

"And what is that?"

"Oh, nothing much really," answered Frederick, reluctant to get into the details of his actual life. "A little of this, a bit of that."

"Like the rest of us," the bartender replied. Tossing the

toothpick into the waste barrel, he turned around and crossed over to the other side of the bar to serve some customers who had just come in, leaving Frederick Linde to his own thoughts.

The story of Itabira made him feel hopeful and miserable at once, hopeful because of its outcome, and miserable because that is what he had set out to do, what his own angel had called him to do, and he had turned that angel down flat for the love of a woman, and who knew, there might have been another woman for him, others, waiting for him in the high Andes or the river jungles where he could have been content, living in a mud hut with a passel of dark-skinned, dark-eyed kids catching river fish with their bare hands while he worked as a laborer on the railroad that would bring life to an entire country. Instead, for failure to heed his soul's calling, for outright refusal, he was sentenced to a bourgeois life not too different from the one he would have done anything to escape, married to a woman whose singular physical beauty was undeniable but whose obstinacy and aloofness was in truth not too different from that of his own mother. He was the father of children whose mediocrity was not too far from his own, condemned to a life of stultifying routine and tortured by the delusion that he was actually helping one living soul by promoting this fool Arts Pavilion to people who would far rather be home going about their own mundane business, whatever that was.

"Damn art," he muttered under his breath, "no good to anyone."

"Never was. A bum from the word go," came a slurred comment from the whiskered man a few stools down.

Frederick Linde hadn't noticed him earlier. He looked at the old man, an obvious barfly, watery eyes, chin almost on chest. He regarded the man for a moment before he realized that the man was making a lame joke and another minute before he had the good grace to laugh. "You're right about that, buddy," Frederick Linde said to him and clapped him on the back.

He put a couple of dollars on the counter and left with the same feeling of distress that brought him here.

He drove out farther along the Olaca road, beyond Oderada, out past the salt plains. Just before the turnoff to the coast highway, where the vista opened up to show an expanse of sky that stretched all the way to Monterrey, Frederick pulled off the road and shut down the engine.

He was quickly cowed by the majesty of the sky. Its sunset colors, its vastness, its staggering stillness overtook him, and, escaping for a moment from the thoughts that pursued him like a pack of dogs, he bowed his head.

At the sight of his hands, though, recriminations rushed at him with renewed vitriol. Soft, long-fingered, uncallused, the hands of privilege. Hands, he realized with continuing gloom, that had never touched dirt out of necessity. Sure, to roughhouse on the lawn with the boys or to help his wife dig the foot-deep hole for a new rosebush, but never because he had to, or others depended on him to. No, he was the kind of man that dreamed up Arts Pavilions in the middle of nowhere. Pavilion. He shut his eyes at the pretentiousness of the word for a small white building, a former warehouse, on the edge of town.

This very evening he would be there, dressed in his

tuxedo, cologned and clean-shaven, auburn hair slicked back to emcee the grand opening. There would be the recital of the Boys' Glee Club from Laredo. An exhibition of landscape paintings of the Texas plains he had begged from the History Center at Zacopa. A mariachi band from Reynosa. Hector Del Burta and his dancers ready to instruct the populace of Santa Rosalia in the stirring steps of the tango.

Frederick Linde rested his head down on the steering wheel wishing to God he had never conceived of the idea, never badgered the town council to restore the building, never agreed to be present at the opening. It was only with the greatest of self-discipline that he sat up and put the key in the ignition. The engine strained, then sputtered and died. He tried again, pumping the gas pedal. There was a half-hearted sputter, then nothing.

Relief flooded Frederick Linde, then panic. His watch said seven o'clock and it was an hour's drive back to Santa Rosalia. He had promised to be there by now, long before now, at six o'clock, five-thirty even, to keep Mrs. Snall from wringing her hands over the leers of the tango dance band and to see to it that the mayor had a two-foot stool so he could appear tall and imposing as he delivered his introduction to the poetry contest, and assure Miss Teldo that the paintings of the oil boom were hung exactly right, and a thousand other inconsequential details.

With a rising sense of alarm, Frederick Linde jumped out of the car to flag down a passerby. The road was more or less deserted.

After a few minutes a paintless pickup whizzed by.

Frederick did not attempt to flag it down.

He leaned against his car and looked up at the sky.

Anyone seeing him might think here was a man with time on his hands, a man who had the sense to stop and luxuriate at the sunset and the coming of evening.

A car passed by. Then another.

Frederick stood with his hands in his pockets, a strange resolve in him growing stronger as each car disappeared down the road.

As the flame of sun sunk below the horizon, Frederick nodded his head as if heeding some inner voice. He climbed into the backseat of his car and, exhausted from his arduous descent into self-pity, fell asleep.

ii.

It was already six-thirty in the evening and I knew there would be a fight. That's why I served dinner at five, to give the señora time to relax. I know how she is when she doesn't want to do something. But now it was time.

I walked into the room with the paintings of the sea at Veracruz, where she sits after dinner.

"Señora," I said firmly. "Señora, it is time to get ready."

The señora put down her sewing and made a face. "Lord in heaven, Concha," she said. "I'm not up to it."

Sometimes she was worse than the children.

"You have to go, señora. How will it look if you stay here stitching your clothes while everyone in town goes to the grand opening of the Arts Pavilion? The Arts Pavilion that your husband built?"

"I don't care," she said flatly.

"You must care. For the sake of the town. And Mr. Frederick."

"Where is he? Why did he not come back for dinner?"

"He said he will meet you at there, at the Arts Pavilion tonight. Remember? He told you himself."

"Ah," she remembered. Then her face went sour. "Oh, why can't people stay home and listen to the radio? There's too much gadding about these days. Music is a private thing. A crowd of people is not necessary to enjoy it," she said with an exasperated sigh. Then as if recalling something of the utmost importance, "Where are the boys?" she asked anxiously.

"Outside playing with the ball. Mr. Xavier is in the library over there reading."

She called to him.

He put his book down and came to stand before her.

"For Lord's sake, Xavier, why are you always moping around the house? You read too much."

"Sorry, Mother." Xavier hung his head. It was pitiful to see, the señora always disapproving of him.

"I was just going out with the others," he lied. Poor thing, such a good boy, but so cautious, afraid almost, but of what? None of us could say. He lived among us, but distant from us, like an animal lurking about the shadows.

"Put that book down and go out with the others. You're too pale as it is," the señora ordered him.

"Yes, Mother. Of course," he said and put his book on the shelf and went to find his brothers.

"And don't be so agreeable," she yelled after him. She turned to me tsk-tsking in disapproval. "He needs some spine," she told me. "Always slinking around here like a scared cat. And he's too serious. Rules, rules, rules. Study, study, study. He has got to come out of his shell. And those gloomy eyes of his. He's seventeen. At that age, I had more gumption in my little finger . . ."

"Yes, señora. Don't you worry about Mr. Xavier. He is getting ready for what calls him," I said to get her mind off her oldest son. "Come on now, let's go upstairs and do your bath," I said. "I'll put in the rose petals." Just like a child, she has to be soothed and coaxed to do something she doesn't want.

She returned to her sewing. "Five minutes."

Still, she took ten, fifteen. Then I had to yell, "Señora! Now! You're worse than the children!" The boys had just come running into the house and heard their mother being scolded. It stopped them and they laughed like hyenas until they saw her with the scowl on her face.

"Outside," she told them. "I'll not have you eavesdropping on me!"

I stood at the top of the stairs with her robe. "Come, I will put your hair up so you can relax in the bath."

"Oh, alright, Concha." She said it in disgust, but she came anyway, right into the bath off their bedroom, letting her clothes stay where they dropped on the floor.

"The trouble with all you people is that you can't stop wanting something from me," she said, climbing into the tub. "This wanting will be your downfall."

"Yes, señora."

While she was in the bath, I went to her closet. There was no preparing beforehand. Her dress always depended on her mood. With the mood she was in, I knew there would be another fight. I put the dress I wanted her to wear at the front of the closet.

But of course, when she finally got out of the bath, she looked right past it.

"I'll take this one," she said, pulling out a black dress with a revealing bosom.

"No, señora, not tonight."

"Then this one," she said, holding a gold chiffon with a full skirt up against her body.

"Not that one either. The people will disapprove."

"For the love of the saints, Concha, what difference does it make? It's Frederick's party. It's him they want to see."

"You are wrong, señora. The people know Mr. Frederick, it's you they want to see, they want to see the woman who gives this man his dreams."

To that she had nothing to say, so I took the moment to pull out the dress I wanted her to wear, a gown with a scooped neck and little capped sleeves and a flowing skirt, a gown the green of a hummingbird's throat.

"This old thing?"

"Yes, señora. It is proper and a little foolish at the same time. It is sharp but with a good heart, after all your mama made it with you in mind." I held it up to her. "Do you see what it does to your eyes? Your hair? In this dress you are a queen."

"Hmmm," was all she had to say. "Should I wear my hair up? Or down?"

"Up, I will fix it for you. With gardenias in the side. Look, I've brought some from the garden."

She sat still like a good child while I did her hair and her makeup, though she didn't need much of that, she was as beautiful as Magdalene, high cheekbones and glowing, lineless skin, just a touch of lipstick and rouge, and never anything around those dark eyes, which were unusual enough to stop the cars in the street.

Such beauty even the señora could not deny. She watched herself in the mirror as I worked, not in a vain way, but watching how she could be transformed from a pouty little girl to a radiant woman, with admiration for the change in what was on the outside and the inside too, for her mood grew softer, the orneriness melting and changing into a yearning for the evening that she was required to attend.

I fastened the South Sea pearls around her neck, the ones Mr. Frederick had given her for one birthday or another. "So beautiful. A string of little moons, señora."

"Yes, aren't they," she said, looking at the pearls in the mirror and absently touching their lustrous round shapes. She sighed a gentle little sigh that said to me that she had left her difficult mood on the other shore.

Now she wanted to talk.

"Do you know what Rosalba Vilar said to me the other day?" she asked me. "She said that if people like Frederick didn't take pity on us, we would fall from God's favor. Isn't that amazing, that they think that of Frederick. He would be cheered."

"You must tell him."

"Yes. You're right. He is feeling, I don't know, sad these days."

"He is just nervous, señora, about the opening of the Arts Pavilion."

"No, Concha, he's not a man whose nerves give out over the gift he's giving to the town. It's something else," she told me, "something that is eating at his heart. I don't know what it is. And if you want to know the truth, it upsets me a little."

At her confession, I began to be afraid myself, for it is not like Mr. Frederick to be dissatisfied with anything. He is the engine that keeps us all going. In his love for the señora he was firm and constant, so it couldn't be that. It struck me that maybe he was sick. If that was it, I promised myself I would find a cure, I would not trust him in the hands of the doctors, I would go back to the old ways of the medicines of my country, the way the señora's grandmother knew them, old Yermina Garzón, she was dead now but when she was alive she took herself into the countryside with the secrets of curing the hopeless. Right then and there, with my back to the señora so she wouldn't see me, I made the sign of the cross and vowed that every morning I would make him drink red clover tea to flush out the poisons in his blood.

She had me worried too, but I didn't want to show her that. So I said in a calm voice, "It's seven-thirty, señora, you'd better be off so you don't keep them waiting on stage."

Now she was the sweetest girl in the world. "You're right, Concha," she called over her shoulder, and with me huffing and puffing behind her, she hurried down the stairs. Even Jesse and Freddie got up from the floor where they were playing with their cards and stood still, swept away by the sight of her.

"Can we come, Mama?" asked Jesse, who always liked a party.

"No, dear boys. It's a dull evening for us dull grown-ups," the señora answered. She gave them each a kiss and sailed out of the house like she couldn't get to where she was going fast enough.

iii.

At eight o'clock, Xavier Linde was sitting in the new auditorium, waiting for the judging of the poetry contest. He wore a white linen suit, just like the suits his father had become known for, carried a pocket watch and a linen handkerchief. His hair was slicked back with Florida water, and for a boy of seventeen he looked like an ancient dandy.

Xavier surveyed the expanse of dark seats in the small auditorium, savoring the fact that in the next fifteen minutes they would be filled with the men and ladies of his town, all dressed in their fine clothes, enjoying an evening they could never have imagined without the work of his own father, and possibly, no probably, listening to the first work by a new and promising poet: himself.

From upstairs came the strains of tango music and the footsteps of what sounded like elephants across the floor. Of all the arts, his father preferred music, but when he conceived the Arts Pavilion, he did not want to impose his preferences on the town. "No art shall want for a home when the pavilion is finished," his father would say.

Finally, the music stopped and people began to drift in, laughing and chatting about the fine evening it all was. The Armisteds walked up the aisle of the auditorium to the back where he was sitting. He looked down at the floor in hopes they wouldn't notice him. Mr. Armisted called his name.

Xavier nodded, knowing that the slight movement of his head wouldn't do. Mr. Armisted was too loud and too nosy for that. "Well hello there, Xavier, you're here early," he called out.

Xavier mumbled a polite hello, remembering how in talking about Mr. Armisted, his father used a word he had never heard: blowhard. Praying they'd move on, he kept his eyes on the program. The Armisteds sat down next to him.

"How's your mother? All ready for the judging tonight?" Mr. Armisted asked in a too-loud voice.

Xavier nodded, hoping Mr. Armisted's voice hadn't reached the surrounding rows that were beginning to fill up with people.

"We think your father is doing a great thing for us here, dear." Mrs. Armisted leaned over and touched his hand. "And your mother too." She smelled of orange cologne.

"Enter a poem, eh Xavier?" Mr. Armisted poked him in the ribs.

Reddening, Xavier tried to laugh it off. "Not the poet sort," he mumbled. "Not me. Just here to lend some family support."

"Good fellow, good fellow." Mr. Armisted clapped him on the back.

Xavier reddened again, remembering the day his father came up with the idea of a poetry contest to launch the Arts Pavilion. He had gotten the idea from a novel he was reading. "Yes, that's it. Just the thing!" he had said, laying down his book in his lap and explaining the idea to the family.

"There are no poets around here," his mother responded.

His father smiled. "You'd be surprised," he consoled her. "We're all poets in our way."

"Bad ones at that."

"Alright," he challenged her. "Just to show you, I propose to name you the person to read the winning poem."

Ayela Linde had let loose with a gale of laughter. "Well, if that's what it takes to convince you that we're not all created equal when it comes to poetry, I will gladly read the heartbreaking attempt of some poor soul with the foolhardiness to write down his not so noble thoughts."

Xavier had seized on that, had not been able to let it go. Like a tongue going to the empty spot left by a pulled tooth, his mind kept visiting and revisiting his father's belief that we are all poets in our own way.

Finally, he knew what he would do to get to his mother.

He would write the winning poem. A great, vivid, intelligent poem about the only woman in the world for him: her. Never having written a poem didn't daunt him. He'd certainly been forced to read enough of them and commit them to memory. The Romantics would be his guide, they could write about anything as though they loved it, a daffodil, a bird, an old urn, and there would not be a reader with a dry eye in the land. His would no doubt be better. After all, he had the more compelling subject, and he would simply write about his mother's attributes, her physical beauty, her irresistible charm, her ways that were as variable as the weather, her impossible unapproachable self. For that is what he felt, what he had always felt, he knew without being told that that was why he was forever howling as an

77

infant. Because she was unavailable, she was unconcerned with him, not bewildered, because that would presuppose care, and she didn't, she was annoyed, exasperated with his little red being howling up at her only wanting the gaze of those magical eyes upon him.

The minute he was old enough to hear Concha tell the story about coming to work for them, Xavier felt vindicated. The first time he heard that story, his festering humiliation had taken on the pain of an open wound. How he had begged Concha to tell and retell the story until he was sure that the situation was crystal clear and he was exactly right about his mother's feelings. Now he recalled the story with a moldering sorrow.

Concha had just come up from her country, eager to find a new life in the land of promise. From Matamoros, where she had worked as a waitress for a time, she had begged her way over the Rio Grande and then begged a ride in the back of a truck carrying grapefruits. The driver dropped her off in Santa Rosalia because he had a girlfriend whose family had a stall selling paper birds in the market in town. A woman selling flowers in the market told Concha about a lady who wanted a housemaid, and she ran all the way to her so happy she was going to a new life. But her heart was heavy when she saw the house, it was large and gleaming white like a palace. "Like the house of a queen, and it frightened me," Concha always liked to say.

Concha forced herself to ring the bell, but she started to run away when a woman opened the door. She was young, perhaps Concha's own age, with beautiful wild black hair and a child in her arms, a little red-faced prune crying as if it might explode. "Pardon," she said. "Pardon, señora, I have no business being here." The lady frowned and shifted the wailing baby from one hip to the other and blew a stray lock of hair up out of her face. "Neither do I," the lady said, and asked her to come in.

And this is the point at which Xavier always began to listen with his whole being.

The three of them, Concha and the señora with her baby, sat in the room just off the black-and-white-checkered entrance and the baby cried so they couldn't hear themselves think. Concha stood up and took the baby from the señora and laid him on his back in her lap with his head on her knees. She rubbed his belly like her mother had done with her brothers and sisters. Just like them, the body of this wailing baby went soft, the crying stopped, and in two minutes he was sleeping. Such a simple thing. The señora didn't smile or thank her or even say she'd hire her. "I'll show you to your room," she said simply. Of course, that baby was himself, baby Xavier, an annoyance to his mother even then and he not smart enough to stop screaming for her attention, her touch, her acknowledgment of his own terrifying existence. Even Concha had seen as much in five minutes.

Xavier excused himself on the pretext of having to find his father, and crawled over the Armisteds to flee to the back of the auditorium, which was now filled. He stood leaning against the back wall with closed eyes, feeling in his heart that he would wake up to his mother's throaty voice reading his poem, the poem he had written for her.

The first sound he heard was the mayor himself, welcoming the ladies and gentlemen of the audience to the first annual poetry contest of the Arts Pavilion of Santa Rosalia. The mayor, a portly sort with an authoritative voice made for public speaking, rambled on about the fine opportunity the Arts Pavilion afforded Santa Rosalia.

Xavier did not see his mother come on stage, because he did not open his eyes. As always, he felt her presence, a knowing elegance, an assured grace, a prickly authority. In the eternity in which it took the form that was his mother to move center stage and open the envelope she was handed by the mayor, Xavier Linde felt himself go mad, stepping forward and clenching the back of the seat in the last row as if it were a lifeline delivering him from the morass of unhappiness.

Finally, her voice sounded. It took a full minute of denial until Xavier ceded the fantasy of what she should be saying, and capitulated to the actual words that were coming from her mouth, words he had never heard, strange dull words about a misty sea, incomprehensible and deeply offensive. All pointing to the reality that once again, her attention was not on him.

He was far from the auditorium by the time she finished the long lyrical piece, which, he found out two days later, was written by Mercedes Comche's cousin, a laundress who was visiting from Matamoros. He staggered out of the Arts Pavilion as though he had been shot in the heart and, moving quickly in a chartreuse-tinged dream of confusion and dejection, floated far away from the sound of his mother's voice. He fled, as fast as he could and not bothering to see who was watching him hurry away. Once out of the building, he broke into a full-fledged run, the night air felt cool

and comforting on his skin, and in his white linen suit
he ran blindly down one street and up the next until he
stopped, panting, in a back alley, crying over his fate, in the
company of the dogs that were fishing through the garbage
pails for the remains of the restaurant food.

Back at home, his brothers were rolling on the floor
laughing over a piece of paper they had found on Xavier's
desk, a handwritten note with some old gibberish about "a
raving black-haired queen, a goddess did he mean, the spirit
of my dreams, a woman cherished more than time."

iv.

Two mornings after the opening of the Arts Pavilion, Felidia
Garzón came into the breakfast room unannounced and sat
down. The boys had gone off to school, and Ayela Linde,
her daughter, was alone in the kitchen. Though Ayela could
detect her mother a mile away, she didn't acknowledge her
presence and busied herself at the sink, washing the breakfast dishes, filling the olive oil bottle, boiling eggs, splitting
the chickens for dinner, whatever she could think of to ignore the woman who had given her life.

Finally, it became too much for the old woman. "Well,
what's the matter?" Felidia Garzón demanded of her
daughter.

"Nothing, Mother."

Felidia Garzón tightened her black shawl about her
shoulders and resettled herself on the breakfast nook bench.
"I can see that something is off in this household. There is a
stink around here. I can smell it. A stink like an animal that

died in the middle of the room and will not move. And no one will tell me why."

"Then maybe it's none of your business," answered her daughter.

Felidia Garzón got up to pour herself a cup of coffee. "It's Frederick's brand of stink. Silent and cold and deadly. It will grow into a great gargantuan black spot and wipe us all out. And we still won't know why."

Ayela Linde said nothing.

"Doesn't he ever yell and scream? Doesn't he ever let anything out? No, he just stinks up the place without saying one single word. One day he's going to drop dead from the rot inside him."

Ayela didn't respond.

"I'm right, you can't deny that," the old woman said, sitting down at the table again.

Ayela stood at the sink with her back to her mother. She went on drinking her coffee and staring straight ahead of her. Not because she didn't agree with her mother, but because of the contentious relationship that began the day she dropped from her mother's womb, a howling prune of a baby, ravenous for milk that had not begun to flow and sucking at the dry breast with a sense that her mother held nothing she needed.

Felidia Garzón took a different tack. "Frederick didn't go to the opening the other night," she said. "After all that work. It must be something awful that kept him away."

Ayela rinsed out her empty cup.

"It doesn't take a witch doctor to know something is up." Felidia Garzón stared at her daughter's back. "Why?"

"Why what?"

"Why didn't he go?"

"We told you, Mother, his car had a flat. He was stranded."

"Why didn't he use the spare?"

Ayela turned around. "I don't know, there probably wasn't one."

"A man as careful as Frederick. That's not like him."

"He said no one came by," replied Ayela Linde, growing more exasperated by the minute. "Otherwise he would have taken a ride with them."

"On the Olaca road? Not another driver on the Olaca road? That's ridiculous."

"So what, Mother?" Ayela crossed the kitchen and stood over her mother with an irritation that crescendoed in a barrage of words. "Maybe he fell asleep in the car. Maybe he wasn't even there. Maybe he drove down to Mexico to screw the cocktail waitresses in the border cafés. Maybe he just didn't feel like going to the damn opening."

"Watch your tongue, young lady," Felidia Garzón scolded her daughter. "I'm still your mother." She smoothed the stray strands of hair that had dared to escape from the bun on her neck and with a stare that bore down on her daughter said, "And I know what I know."

"And what is that, Mother?"

Felidia Garzón allowed herself a little smile. "That you are living with a man who desperately needs to get out from under this blasted household."

Ayela managed a laugh. "He's barely here anyhow. He's always working, and when he's not working he's running around building this, that, and the other thing all over town."

"It's not his job to be here," Felidia Garzón told her daughter. "A man's place is not in the house, tending to dirty dishes and scraped knees."

"Oh really. And you know what he needs, I'm sure."

"Yes," answered Felidia Garzón. She waited quietly, patiently, considering the veins that stood out on her ancient hands.

"Well?"

Felidia looked up. "He needs to finish what he started."

"And what might that be?"

"What he came here for. To leave." Felidia Garzón delivered her observation with pleasure. "Before you stopped him."

Ayela Linde's mouth tightened and her chin stuck out. "If you remember correctly, it was Frederick who followed me around like a whiny goat, begging me to marry him." At the time, Ayela couldn't for the life of her understand the ferocious attentions of Frederick Linde, whose dallying in the dirt streets of Santa Rosalia with his auburn good looks and obvious breeding seemed to her a blasphemous waste, though he dismissed her doubts right to her face with a lovesick look and the statement, "I am no longer a free man." She had been on the verge of refusing him altogether, but as she told Rosalba Vilar over lemonade the afternoon before she eloped, "I can't bear to think of him using the same lines on another girl."

Wisely, Felidia Garzón let that irrefutable argument drop. She had bigger fish to fry. Leaning forward on the table and lowering her voice, she dealt the deathblow. "That article in the paper about the railroad in Brazil," she began. "You think I do nothing but sit in my chair and weep for the past. But I see things. I'm not blind yet. And I saw that little article about the railroad in Brazil. Even before I finished reading the whole thing, I knew what it would start over here, in this very house." She paused for effect, and then started in again. "I knew Frederick would see the article. I knew he would want to go. He's a do-gooder, just like your father. Those men, they have dreams. They can't stay put. It's not in their nature."

"Just because you couldn't keep a man for more than twenty-four hours," Ayela snapped, referring to the accident of her own birth.

The insult did not faze Felidia Garzón. "That's right," she replied. "I knew better. But you. You can't for the life of you see why your husband is in such a state."

They fumed at each other in silence.

Finally the old woman stood up. "Well, I can see I'm doing no good here," she said. "But before I leave I'm going to set you straight." She shook her finger like an old witch. "That man of yours wants to keep doing what he set out to do. Before you stopped him." She repeated the accusation with a kind of gleeful maliciousness. "And he will get away, one way or another." With that, she pushed her coffee cup to the center of the table and rose without another word.

In the doorway Felidia Garzón stopped and turned around to face her daughter. "You listen to an old woman," she warned Ayela Linde with an ominous eye. "Living with a man whose spirit is somewhere else will send you running to your grave."

No sooner had the front door closed behind her mother than Ayela Linde sprang up from the table and, seizing the cleaver, began to hack at the dinner chickens until the fragile bones splintered and a torrent of lacerated legs and thighs and wings and breasts flew off the kitchen counter and onto the floor. She kept at it like a madwoman, letting out a string of curses that made Concha come running in from the garden.

"Señora, what is it? What has happened?"

Ayela Linde offered no explanation. With a distant look in her eye, she laid down her cleaver and, without surveying the mess she had created, stepped out of the kitchen. "When Frederick comes in, tell him I'm waiting upstairs to speak to him."

v.

I almost didn't want to get up the next morning to see what had happened. I told Mr. Frederick the minute he came in. "Sounds serious," he said in that playful way of his. But he went right up to her. They didn't come down to dinner, the boys were asking me why. "Why? They're together," I told them, "thank God for that, have some more chicken and don't think about it."

It was not a bad silence that was coming from their room. Something large and different and hard to say what it was. We all looked up from the table when we thought we heard sobs. There was no yelling or loud voices coming from their room, perhaps there was love but it didn't feel like it, just a long low tenseness like an elastic being stretched as far as it could go.

The children went up to bed without seeing their mama and papa. That was a first for them in all these years, not seeing one or the other. Xavier and Freddy were big boys, boys with other things on their minds, but Jesse, he was still young enough to come to my room in his pajamas, and cry. "Concha, can I stay with you? But don't tell anyone," he said, not wanting the other boys to know he was scared, though he himself didn't know the reason for his fear.

"Of course," I said, and pulled back the covers and hugged him to me because I had just the same feeling as he did. For I loved my life in this house and my life depended on everything staying the way it had always been, on both the señora and Mr. Frederick going on the way they always had.

And then in the morning I woke at five as usual, started the coffee and the eggs and the fresh bread and went about my business setting the table and fixing the tray; the señora and Mr. Frederick take their first morning coffee upstairs, it is their private time. When I hear them begin to move about, I leave the tray, always arranged with a cabbage rose, outside the room. But no one goes to them until they have bathed in the mosaic shower with the fish-mouth faucets and pulled their clothes from closets that smell of sandalwood and the señora has sat down at her dressing table and done her hair and added a woman's touch to the placing of the onyx pin in the silk tie of her husband and to the flaring of the monogrammed handkerchief in his breast pocket and they themselves open the mahogany double doors to their bedroom.

But this morning, before I had time to bring up the tray, Mr. Frederick came down. From the corner of my eye I could see he was wearing the white linen suit, just like always, and whistling the same four-note tune. When I looked up he came at me, "Good morning, Concha," lifting me up and twirling me around. "What a day," he said, on his face was good cheer, for everyone in the world, and he said, "The señora will be down shortly, I've got to pick a rose." He went out into the garden, which is something he never does. He looked like the happiest man alive, so I began to relax, thinking that whatever had been bad between them had been solved.

The señora came in wearing her blue satin robe and slippers, which was a surprise because in the mornings she always comes downstairs dressed. She noticed I looked away when I saw her wearing the robe. "There's going to be a new regime around here," she said, but not in a harsh way, it seemed she might even be glad. What she meant I could not imagine, and I did not want to ask.

Mr. Frederick gave her the rose, a white cabbage rose with light pink edges around the petals.

"How lovely," the señora said.

"It's nothing next to you," said Mr. Frederick. I had not heard him be so toward her in a long time. I wanted to cover my ears, but then what do you know, they embraced right in front of me. What could I do with my eyes?

"Sorry, Concha," Mr. Frederick said. "We're just a little giddy today."

"Yes, Mr. Frederick," I mumbled. I was happy for them, of course, but not completely because there was some strange electricity in the air. I hurried away to finish the eggs and the toast and percolate the coffee, which was something they liked to drink immediately after it was made and not one minute later.

The older boys had forgotten about the night before and the absence of the parents. But not Jesse. He ran right up to his parents and into their arms. Mr. Frederick lifted Jesse up into the air and swung him around, just as he'd done with all the boys when they were small. They were all sweetness and light again, anyone could see that.

Then right away, Jesse ran to his seat at the breakfast table and took to arguing with his brothers about whose toast was better, whose pencil sharper, whose homework was harder, who had the meaner teachers, all of which was ignored by their mother and father. Mr. Frederick read the paper and the señora scribbled lists on her calendar.

In other words, everything was back to normal.

When the meal was half over, Mr. Frederick stood up. He looked nervously at his pocket watch and gave all of us around the breakfast table a strange kind of look. "I know you have to run off to school in a few minutes, so I want all of you to listen carefully to me. You as well, Concha." I stopped pouring the juice and stood still. In my wildest dreams I wasn't ready for what he said to us.

"I'm going to say something now that none of you may like," he said in a serious way. "That no one may like. But I'm going to say it anyway, and I'm going to do it." He began to tell them about the trip he had always wanted to make to a far-away place where life wasn't as easy as it is here in some ways, and that he was going to do what he could in the ways he knew how to make things a little easier, a little safer, a little less of a problem. "Not that the physical world is ultimately that important," he said. "But it is what we face every day."

That was Mr. Frederick, always throwing in a line or two that no one understood.

The boys didn't realize what that meant, I could see from their squirming and staring off. But what Mr. Frederick said next went straight through their outer shells.

"I am going to be away for one year," he said, like it was a precious gift he had just received and would never grow tired of.

Questions came spurting from the boys like a volcano. Why? When? Where? What was the point? All of which he answered in a calm voice.

"It's impossible," said Freddie; his lips began to tremble just a bit.

"When are you going?" asked Jesse. "When?"

"Well, as soon as I can wrap up some work here and make plans," Frederick went on. "In less than a month's time, I suspect."

"Papa, can I come? I want to go away too," Jesse insisted, like his father was taking a trip to the ice-cream shop.

Still, Jesse's eagerness to go pleased Mr. Frederick. "Ah, Jesse, I wish you could," he said, with a thread of regret in his voice. "Someday you will do as I am doing, but not yet."

Freddie took it the worst of anyone. A storm was gathering over his face and all of a sudden he jumped up and began to stomp away. "Father, I know what you're doing. You're throwing Mother over," he cried. "How could you?"

Frederick ran after him and took him by the shoulders. "Your mother has generously agreed to let me go," he told him.

The señora smiled.

"But that's what everyone will think. That you've left us," Freddie wailed.

"Is it true? Is it true?" Jesse threw his napkin into his eggs on his plate and started to wail too.

"Who will help us? Who will come to my school meetings? Who will help me with my mathematics?" Freddie moaned. His body shook with sobs in his father's arms.

Freddie and Jesse cried louder.

In all the commotion, Mr. Frederick began to look weak. "I'm sorry to leave your mother without help," he said. "That is the one thing that gives me pause."

The breakfast room was quiet except for the sobs of the boys.

Then the señora got up from her place at the table. She went to stand behind Xavier. Like it was the most natural thing in the world, she put her arms around his neck, she kissed his cheek, and ran her hand affectionately over the auburn hair that was worn with a side part, just like his father's. "But I am not without help," she announced. "You will be the man of the house, won't you, my love?" she said to Xavier.

During the whole scene, Xavier had remained calm. He was listening to his father and his brothers fussing, I could see that; his eyes, more serious even than his father's, were taking it all in. But no complaints came from him. He ate his eggs and drank his café con leche as if it were a typical morning. That the señora had singled him out was sure to make him crazy with happiness, that much I knew. Yet it was hard to tell what was going through his mind. He kept on chewing.

"Of course, Mother, of course I will," he said finally with that sober expression of his that now seemed to comfort everyone in the family. "You can count on me."

8

The Waning Moon of Aurelio Almengar

1960

At six o'clock, my husband Aurelio Almengar, a simple man, a man of habit, strode through the front door in his sand-colored suit, wearing the rimless spectacles inherited from his maternal grandfather. Under his arm was the green ledger that all day, every day, was spread out on the gray metal desk in his office right next to the mayor's, where he kept watch over the accounts as if one dollar unwisely spent would plunge the town of Santa Rosalia into eternal ruin. He had no formal training for the job, but it suited his temperament and he was fond of saying of himself, "Once poor, never rich, and that's why the mayor has me running this show."

At seven o'clock, when he had changed his clothes and laid out his pad and his pencils, sharpened and arranged in size order to be taken up again later, my husband joined me in the dining room to eat the tasteless soup prepared by Jula, our cross-eyed housekeeper who ran around barefoot like a child in a mud hut.

We ate in silence. Music floated over from the house next door. The neighbor boy, Stefan, was practicing the piano in a melody that rushed in and retreated like the tide. He often played at this time of evening, giving our plain dinners a kind of sad beauty.

The music was interrupted by Jula's high-pitched voice. "Mr. Frederick Linde wants to see you."

"Tell him I haven't come in yet," Aurelio said.

Jula returned. "Mr. Linde says he can hear you slurping the soup you eat every night of your life. He says he'll wait until you're ready to see him."

My husband went on eating. "Let him wait, then. And tell him he's not going to get another dime out of me for those cockamamie projects of his."

The music stopped, and Jula could be heard repeating those very words to Mr. Linde in the hall. She returned with a puzzled expression. "He says if you let him sit there too long he's going to have time to think about building an opera house."

"Museums, opera houses. What for? If Mr. Linde has to have all those fancy things, he ought to go back to Boston."

"Yes," I agreed. My husband had no use for the niceties of life. But he turned sixty-three last month, and I don't bother myself anymore about his likes and dislikes.

Frederick Linde himself appeared in the doorway. "Good evening, señora," he said, bowing to me. "Forgive me for barging in."

94

What surprised me was how immaculate his light linen suit was at the end of the day. He looked like a man who came from somewhere cool and comfortable and without difficulties. He was younger than Aurelio, in his late forties, with red-gold hair and his own teeth. My husband considered him an adversary, though Mr. Linde seemed incapable of enmity. He appeared to be interested in Aurelio for reasons of his own, and there was an eagerness about him that made me feel tired to the bone.

Aurelio remained hunched over his soup like a truck driver. "You're not going to get another dime out of the town coffers," he said.

I cringed at my husband's crudeness, but Mr. Linde did not take offense. "So I heard. But that's not why I'm here," he said. He exchanged a few pleasantries with me about the October heat before his voice trailed off to an obtuse silence that signaled he would not divulge the reason for his visit in my presence. I withdrew to the parlor just off the dining room, keeping the door ajar, so as to be able to hear. They were quiet so long I thought they had both fallen asleep.

Finally, Frederick Linde spoke. "You're in ill health," he said to Aurelio.

"Yes, I am," Aurelio admitted, through a mouthful of salt roll. "What of it?"

"Nothing. I wanted to know if I could be of help."

Aurelio ignored his offer. "You should be home with your wife."

"She urged me to call on you," Mr. Linde said.

"Oh come now, Mr. Linde," my husband replied. This is a small town, and Aurelio and I have known Ayela Linde since she was a young girl first come into bloom, parading through streets taken by her own beauty. She must be more than forty-five now, and still she has that sense of self-absorption about her, so that my husband, and rightly so I must admit, was incredulous that she had taken notice of his situation.

Mr. Linde caught his inference. He started slowly. "Ayela isn't what you think." He sighed, and I sensed he was weary of having to explain his wife to the people she grew up with. Then he began again. "Now, can I be of help to you?"

I felt Aurelio stare him in the face. "Can you turn back time?"

Mr. Linde let out a small rueful laugh. "No, but I know some excellent physicians," he said.

Aurelio kept his eyes on his soup. "I don't need a doctor to tell me what I already know," he said quietly, and I wondered if Mr. Linde didn't have a magical talent for defeat at the hands of my husband.

That no one else knew of Aurelio's illness was no accident. From the moment his body revealed to him its pitiable state, Aurelio vowed to endure his fate without so much as a minor variation in the route he walked to his office on the second floor of the town hall. He escaped there every day, closing the door behind him and turning his eyes, heavy with the weight of sleepless nights, to the numbing refuge of work. My husband tells me he still gives dictation every morning at eight forty-five to his secretary, Yolana, who receives it with the same bored insolence she has always shown. The mayor still barges in without knocking to drag him off to sound the voice of caution at the barbarous meetings of the town council. The boy who brings his rice and fried meat on a covered plate at lunchtime still sits patiently as Aurelio chews each morsel deliberately, bemoaning that no one knows how to fry meat like his mother, who learned how to cook from the girls in the cantinas of the border towns on the other side of the Rio Grande.

Was it pride that made Aurelio go on as if nothing had happened? Or the grace to accept the unacceptable? All I know is that he has resigned himself, and because of that, so have I.

Aurelio's answer must have put Mr. Linde at a loss for words because it was a time before he spoke again, and when he did his voice had lost some of its luster. "Isn't there something I can do?"

"There are two things you can do," Aurelio told him. "Go home to your wife and don't say a word to anyone. The only thing I can stand less than pity is curiosity."

Later that night I was sitting at my dressing table patting my face with cold cream. In the mirror I could see Aurelio stretched out on the bed, snoring softly. Stefan was playing the piano again, such a lovely melody rising upward toward the moonlight that my eyes closed and my voice followed the music softly.

Aurelio suddenly rose up on his elbows. "Doesn't he ever stop plunking that thing?"

I took a ribbon from the drawer and tied my hair up at the neck and went to fluff up his pillows.

"Ah, that's better," he said. He had a sip from the water

glass on the nightstand and made a face. "Nothing tastes right anymore."

I sat on the bed beside him, but turned toward the window to avoid those poor dying eyes of his. "That was nice of Frederick Linde to look in on you," I told him.

"He's working me over."

"Offering you a good doctor? The man brings you a gift."

"He's always trying to give me something I don't want."

Aurelio slid over toward the middle of the bed. "Now come on, Mama, forget Mr. Linde. Give me a little help here," he said and pulled me down next to him and led my hand down to where he was alive. His breath was in my ear. "Remember how our little parties used to last all night?"

In a determined and joyless way he had his party, and afterwards he sat for several moments on the edge of the bed with his head in his hands. Was there any reason for him to ever move from that position? I thought not, but then he felt among the bed linens for his pajamas, which he put on with great difficulty and went downstairs to sleep on a mat in the kitchen so I wouldn't hear him wrestle all night with his pain.

On Wednesdays the market in the plaza began at dawn. I went early, before seven o'clock.

As I walked by the courthouse, Mr. Linde called my name, and so I stopped to chat, in spite of the feeling that he had singled me out for a reason. He was again dressed in that cream-colored linen suit, and that gave him the radiant appearance that inspired awe in Santa Rosalia. But at that moment there was an unfamiliar urgency about him.

As I suspected, Mr. Linde inquired after my husband. "I hope you left him sleeping like a baby."

"Oh no," I told him. "He's gone off to Mass."

Mr. Linde seemed surprised. "Has he always been such a churchgoer?"

"Always," I said.

I felt myself being examined from head to toe.

"How bad is it?" Mr. Linde asked.

"He doesn't complain. So it's bad." I told him it had been going on six months now. It started with the smell. When Aurelio came in the room, sometimes I caught a bad odor, his breath I thought at first, or not having bathed, but it was something else, like a whiff of rotten meat. Then the set of his mouth, as though he had winced at something and time had frozen his face. In the end, it was the dreams that convinced me. He always told me what he dreamed about, elephants, a green house, his mother's wedding. I hadn't heard for a while and when I asked him why, he said, "Because I don't sleep anymore."

After I told him all this, Mr. Linde frowned. "We've got to get him to a doctor."

"You have to understand," I said, "my husband isn't like that." I looked Mr. Linde full in the face and told him what everyone in Santa Rosalia had known since Aurelio's grandfather had been shot in the town square by an errant bullet meant for a mad dog. Dripping with blood, he had waved away anyone who crossed his path, crawling the quarter mile back to the house of his birth, which was bolted from the inside by his mother who rocked in her chair pining for the

Caribbean breezes of her youth. After three knocks at the heavy door, he expired in a heap on the dirt before she returned from her dreams. "The Almengars don't take help very easily," I explained to Mr. Linde. "And you can see where that's gotten them."

Several days later, after dinner Aurelio came to me and asked me to change my dress. "Put on that green dress with the buttons," he said. It seemed impossible to me that we would be going out, but I went upstairs to change and fix my hair and put a little rosewater on my wrists. When I came down, Aurelio was pacing by the door like a dog with bad weather coming. I asked no questions about where we were going. With his hand at my elbow, steering me, we walked into the night air, down Dolorosa Street and into the Hotel del Norte.

The back parlor on the first floor had been set up as a meeting room. Immediately I recognized Mr. Linde, who was standing before all the important people of Santa Rosalia, speaking of his grand plans for an amphitheater out on the Olaca road.

Mr. Linde was at ease at the podium, pointing with a stick at the drawing of a pretty amphitheater that would host all manner of musical shows. To my mind it was one of those imaginative flights of fancy that would never make it to brick and mortar. Mr. Linde had no such qualms. "This theater will mark a new era for Santa Rosalia," he said in such a knowing voice that it brought a burst of applause from the audience.

They were about to break for refreshments when my

husband went to the podium. "I hope you'll allow me a few words," he said and began to speak in a serious and impassioned tone to the audience, most of whom he had known since they were boys playing marbles in the dirt. "The day there are people listening to a band of kids yelping and gyrating their hips in that hole dug out of the mud is not the day you say hello to a new Santa Rosalia," he said in a grave voice. "It's the day you can kiss Santa Rosalia good-bye. Do I make myself clear?"

No one responded, but he had their attention, even their interest, and he walked over to the easel that held the drawing and turned it around, so all that remained of Mr. Linde's marvelous amphitheater was the black backing of the cardboard on which it was drawn. Without even a smile to soften things up, Aurelio began to speak of the ten, the hundred, the thousand things that Santa Rosalia needed more than an outdoor music hall.

"Besides," he said. "There's no greater music than the sound of a quiet night in a small town."

He said all that before he had one of his fits of pain that seemed always to start in his stomach and radiate around to his back. When he began to lose his footing, Mr. Linde and another man in the first row rushed to steady him. Ignoring Aurelio's protests, they walked him into the hotel lobby, where they sat him in the largest chair in the house and put his feet up on a hassock. By the time I got to him, he was resting his head on the back of the overstuffed chair. "When I wake up," he murmured drowsily, "remind me to tell them that for the price of that damned music hall, we could build a sewer lined with gold."

Mr. Linde sat on the other side of Aurelio, watching him doze with the worried air of a new mother. When Aurelio woke twenty minutes later, Mr. Linde insisted on driving us the two blocks from the Hotel del Norte to our house.

There was not another car like his in Santa Rosalia. It was a new model and a shining silver color, with seats of fresh red leather. So smoothly did it ride that it could have been a ship moving silently on the still night water.

To show that his illness had not got the better of him, Aurelio asked Mr. Linde to come in for a brandy. I took the brandy in to them on a tray. Aurelio drank it in two swigs, but Mr. Linde lingered over his, and they spoke together in low tones that seemed to be civil if not congenial until the door sounded and Aurelio called out to me to bring him what the grocer's son had come to deliver.

My husband took the small brown packet and, ripping open the flap, began to pour the contents of the package out into his hand.

Mr. Linde asked him what it was.

"Fennel seeds," Aurelio told him. "Better than the analgesic pills."

Mr. Linde frowned. "What nonsense. For God's sake," he said. "I know the top doctor in Laredo. I've already spoken to him, and I'm going to drive you over there myself on Wednesday." He grabbed the packet from Aurelio, and whether he meant it to happen or not, the seeds dropped out and scattered over the floor.

I started to go out of the room. "Stay where you are, Mama," he said to me. "Mr. Linde can make an idiot of himself in front of you too."

Aurelio grew flushed. "This 'nonsense' has the recommendation of hundreds of years of use," he said, stepping forward until he was a hand's breadth from Mr. Linde. "Tell me one thing before I throw you out of here," he said into the poor man's face. "Why the devil are you haranguing me about all this?"

Mr. Linde got up and walked over to the small corner table and put his hands on the back of the chair. His eyes closed, and he remained silent for a long time. "I don't know," he said finally, shaking his head. "Maybe I can't stand to see foolishness."

"You see foolishness every day of your life," Aurelio said.

"But not from a smart man."

Aurelio put his hands in his pockets. He walked closer to his opponent and said in a lowered voice, "You know, one would think it's you whose time was up here." Mr. Linde started to protest but Aurelio cut him off with a look and continued speaking in a tone that had become cold and challenging: "Don't worry so much, Mr. Linde. This kind of thing doesn't happen to people like you." Aurelio snickered and shook his head. "Anyway, it's only a matter of a rotting body. And one can't be too attached to the body."

Mr. Linde was going to storm away, I could feel it. He took a few angry steps toward the door, but he stopped in the middle of the room. His wrath seemed to melt away. He stood still and kept his eyes lowered for several moments, and when he raised them again he looked as if he had come back from the deepest part of himself. He looked at Aurelio with an expression of confused loneliness. "What a stupid shit I am," he said.

"Not a shit," Aurelio said. "Just stupid."

Frederick Linde broke into a soft smile. "Just stupid," he repeated.

I thought that was the last we would see of Mr. Linde. For a few months there was no sign of him, and we didn't mention his name. On a Thursday evening in March, Jula came into the yard where we were sitting under the trees playing canasta, and announced that Mr. Linde was here to take us for a drive.

We got into the silver car without protest and drove out of town on the old road that ran through the citrus groves that were in the height of their bloom. I thought we might drown in the scent of those blossoms. It was a scent I remember even now.

Out past town on the Olaca road, just at the old rock promontory, Mr. Linde pulled off the road and shut down the engine.

We could see that the old rock had been transformed to a shrine of some sort.

"Oh, for Christ sakes," Aurelio said. "You had to go and build something."

"Don't worry, I paid for it out of my own pocket."

"Good," Aurelio said.

Mr. Linde told him it was modeled after the grotto at Lourdes. "Right down to the look in the Virgin's eye," he said with pride.

"Really? I wouldn't know."

"So I'm telling you," Mr. Linde said, hopping out of the car to come around and open the door for Aurelio and me.

"Your wife's idea, no doubt," Aurelio said, climbing out of the front seat with a sour expression.

As soon as Aurelio said that, I knew it was true. Ayela Linde had a lifetime of such beliefs, her grandmother running around town with her potions and spells, her mother kneeling at the altar of the Church of San Lorenzo every day of her life. Mr. Linde didn't have such things in him, and he didn't dignify Aurelio's accusation with a response.

Instead, he led us over the footbridge that spanned the small stream and around the stand of mesquite trees to the grotto, which rose in a heap of jagged rocks. In the hollow of the rock face stood the statue of the Virgin with that vague smile. The spot was dark and deeply quiet. In the air was that faintly metallic smell of earth after a rainfall. The beauty of it sent me to my knees at once, but not Aurelio. He went up to the rock and touched it. For a few moments he disappeared around back, and then returned. From the corner of my eye I saw him pacing impatiently, and soon he went to the car to wait for us.

I remained kneeling with my head bowed until the stones under my knees grew too much for me. Mr. Linde helped me to my feet and we walked back without a word.

"Lourdes, indeed," Aurelio said with a scowl when Mr. Linde and I came toward him. "The only miracle about this place will be if we all don't come down with malarial fevers from the damned mosquitoes out here."

As far as I know, after that night Aurelio and Frederick Linde never spoke of the illness again. Aurelio died seven months later. During those long months, while he was still able, there were times he came home from the office at six o'clock and, refusing dinner, took the keys to the car from the brass hook by the door. "I'm going for a little drive, Mama," he would tell me. "Where?" I would ask, and he would take off his spectacles and rub them clean with his handkerchief and answer, "Oh, just a drive, in the car, on a road."

On those nights I sat alone at the dining table listening to Stefan make the evening weep with the melancholy beauty of his piano. Darkness came on and still I sat at the table, waiting for Aurelio to return. Hours would pass before his step sounded in the hall. I confess that I sat there cursing Mrs. Linde and her meddling husband, for I knew, I always knew, when Aurelio had been out to that damned shrine. Those were the nights he came home with the noxious smell of hope on his clothes.

9
The Gift of Softened Eyes
1965

The crickets had gotten into the car during the afternoon and were still singing when we arrived at the whitewashed house with the orange tile roof. A little mansion, a jewel hidden in the dark leather-leafed trees. In the stifling air we walked up the slate steps past luxuriant looming shrubs, like two dirty-faced waifs with grass in our hair from sleeping on the ground, like this we had come to sacrifice our lives before they had even begun. He was a little afraid of her; I had inherited his fear but mine was different and because of her beauty. If only she hadn't been beautiful. Beauty was the truth of her, but there was another truth beyond the first, and not even he could have prepared me. A beauty of mixed origin belonged to this woman dressed in white and holding a bowl of oranges who came to see who was at her door, a remote intelligence inhabiting the eyes. What hour can it be in your life when you have both the look of a lost young woman and, with the slight turn of a head, a worn-out drone, this half-breed who could grab a hen under her arm and twist its neck without a thought as easily as she could lead a titled gentleman in a waltz, who puts a jarful of cut onions on her nightstand to cure her insomnia and sees her dead grandfather rustling the altar flowers and speaks only of the impatient expression on his face, this woman who received us with a look of suspicion, as if we were going to rob the place, the two of us hot and dusty from two thousand miles in the blue Beetle that brought us, the unwashed, to her, my hair long and middle-parted and at the slightest nod of my head hanging forward to cover my distaste at being sentenced to this godforsaken town, certain of my inability to ever address this woman by the blessed name of mother.

The father, Frederick, came to investigate the commotion, a tall, slender man with an open heart and the grace of a fencing master. We told them our news, that we had been married by a divinity student at sunset on the Boston Common and were here to settle, near them. She stiffened, eyes freezing over, mouth contracting, but why when the others had broken her heart by moving away from her, first the oldest son ran from her unwitting arrogance, holding his pride like a wounded soldier, and the youngest, her favorite, threw her love away on a diner waitress who smoked thin cigars, and ran too, ran to join his brothers, all of them like homing pigeons, returning by some misguided internal rudder to the Boston their father had abandoned when he was no older than they were. Only Freddie, my lovely Freddie, the middle son, the only one with the stomach for her, the heart to overlook her shortcomings, to return to this stinking hot hellhole of the town of his birth with his future stuffed away like last week's grocery list in his back pocket so she could have her boys again, her family, her hope, so she didn't have to resort to painting birds or playing solitaire or teaching the poor to read. Oh, but the father was a dream, "Congratulations, a stupendous surprise for us, come let me show you the house," he said, offering me his arm, "you see it was built by a general from the Mexican War for his bride, a descendant of the nobility of Cartagena back when there were such things, heh heh, there's the Austrian piano she bought to soothe his restlessness, out there the bower where he retired in the afternoons in dress uniform, closing his eyes to relive his military victories with the climbing roses and the green jays, just imagine," he sighed, "anything grows here, drop a grapefruit seed out the window and the next day a tree has shot up in the quiet which is so still you can hear your thoughts taking shape, perfect for the people of this town who are simplicity itself, too simple some would say, but the way I see it, just simple enough to live life properly, yes, yes," he broke off to watch a lizard run up the wall, a quiver in his voice, "I love it here, you know, I could never go back." Then the mother again, with my Freddie's arm locked in her own, searching us out to deliver her verdict on the unexpected arrival of her second-born and his new bride: "There will be a party, of course, but you'll have to dress for it," she said and left us immediately to begin the furious preparations in which immaculate floors were scrubbed, covered dishes unearthed from storage closets, silver service polished, strings of colored lights hung everywhere, gargantuan roasts split and rubbed with garlic and stuffed and sent off to the spit the grill the oven so the house smelled like heaven and her, the mother, collapsing in a kitchen chair gossiping in Spanish to the servants while

they folded a hundred white linen napkins into the shape of
swans while we looked on from outside, staring at her from
the window, holding hands like two orphans excluded from
the party before the party, watching her profile, listening to
her listen to the sad story of the full-cheeked kitchen maid,
the dissonant music of jealousy beginning to invade me, can't
she see it's me who needs her, and Freddie coming close to my
ear, "Ah, you see, I told you she'd get to you." "I'll take her
now, Mister Freddie," it was Concha, the most trusted of the
servants, the one who had been with Freddie since birth, she
took me from the house through the town with its square and
its limestone church and that impossible light, golden yet rose,
like an old Mexican town but not really, full of fan palms and
zigzag streets where vegetables were sold from stands and
cloth from the back of trucks and Milagro the farmer gave his
carnations to the restaurants in exchange for garbage to feed
his hogs. How I knew those stories. "Oh, Concha, where are
we going in this unbelievable heat?"

"The señora, she's got her ideas," Concha replied, turning down an alley and knocking at a heavy door. An old
woman leaned out the upstairs window scowling, "What is
it, what do you want?" "The grandmother, Mister Freddie's
grandmother," Concha whispered impatiently in my ear,
yes of course the old dressmaker with the widow's hump
and the watery eyes gone nearly blind from too much close
work, she signaled to come in and unlocked a fading
wardrobe and shuffled through stacks of frothy dresses,
picking for me the frothiest, parrot green with spangles,
"No I couldn't possibly, not the blue either, or the pink, well
the yellow perhaps, if you insist."

In the end I wore my own, without froth, straight and simple as a shroud, with a gardenia in my hair that Freddie swiped from a vase on the demi-lune table in the hall just before we entered the party where we were pressed with good wishes and curious gifts by guests who dined on turkey stuffed with apricots and plums and a suckling pig, drinking all there was in the house and then some. She the mother in her ivory dress with the heavy skirts and the moonstone diadem, moving among the guests, introducing us around, to the mayor, to the barber, to her childhood friend, to the owner of the largest citrus grove, bragging about our youth, our handsomeness, our Ivy League degrees, our knowledge of the body's tiniest cells and the stars beyond Pluto, "They're geniuses, these two," and, putting her hand on my head, "If I'd known I'd have a daughter-in-law like this, I'd have gone to school myself," but not a word about our plans to settle here, not one word.

How they loved her, this woman who wore privacy like a mark across her brow even as she flitted like an Amazonian butterfly from the grand room to the patio set up with blue lanterns and a three-piece band playing the lively music of these parts. "Dance, dance," she waved at her guests, the luxuriant hair on top of the head, the face radiant. "Oh my, Frederick," she let herself be twirled, insisting everyone have more turkey, more cakes, more homemade candies of almond paste ground from the nuts that fell from the trees you're sitting under. "Oh, señora, you know how to give a party," they laughed and drank and began to dance themselves so that it seemed a dream and then a dream of a dream, these peculiar strangers embracing us and yet benignly indifferent to us, our youth, our brilliance, glad to have an excuse for an exquisite party on a starry night, circling about in their magnificent anachronistic gardenia-scented world in the cyanic glow of the lanterns so that Freddie, my lovely Freddie, seemed the least of it, right up until the hour that the party wound down like a clock out of time and we were left to ourselves in the sadder-than-death wake of something like this for which the only antidote is sleep.

Oh, Concha, what is it now, why are you shaking me awake at one, two, four o'clock, who knows the hour? "The señora wants you," she whispered over Freddie's snores, and led me through the darkened house that belied the evening's festivities, past the birds asleep in their cages, past the pots of herbs growing noiselessly, out onto the patio where she sat, a woman erect and lovely, in a white nightdress, "Good evening, señora." Without even a greeting, an apology for this middle-of-the-night summons, she turned her icecap eyes on me, berating me for letting her son indulge in this foolishness, this, this charity mission to come back to her, "I never acquired the vice of taking things I don't need," she said sternly, then sighing, drifting, and with a few thin threads of voice admitting, "Well, yes, there might have been a time," the air thinning to make way for the flood of memory, for the ravaged face of her younger self, the architecture of her hair, the pins, the tortoiseshell combs that caught it as it rose off the forehead and twisted it flat against the back of the head, the painstaking effort in the mornings to confine the wild mass of it, the time taken to forestall the moment she would have to step from her bedroom into a house as still as death, a house devoid of squabbling voices, footsteps crashing down stairs, a house whose stale silence fostered her age-old fears: how to fill the minutes of the day, what to think about, want to do, do, how to make the hours pass suitably, longing for the night, the day, the night again.

"And so you would settle here with me," she mused, "I hadn't known about Freddie's heart . . . or yours," and my breath caught from the unexpected gentleness of it and then again from her instructions for the care of her son, "Now take him back where he belongs and don't let him think ill of himself," yes ma'am, "in fact, don't let him think too much at all, it makes him morose," yes ma'am, "take the book from his hands in bed or he'll sleep the night through in that position," yes ma'am, "make him understand that there is such a thing as love without thanks," yes Mother, she went on but I could only look at her eyes, not the languid hand on the chest or the weak lips beginning to tremble, but the eyes, soft and wide as an infant's roaming over the ground and the sky and the bugs and the roses and me as if she were surprised and moved, so very moved that we had all gone to so much trouble for her.

10
The Wooden Swan
1975

Pepillo

I am a man who fears God, a man who takes what he gets as his just reward, not a violent man or one who wishes another harm, but that Mrs. Linde, I'd take a knife to her if I had half a chance. Turning us upside down like that. Three days was all it took her to tear my life apart. Monday she pulled into the gas station. I remember, because of the silver car she drove. No car like that ever stops here. She had on sunglasses and a scarf over her hair, like a movie star. She asked me to fill it up. She spoke to me in Spanish, which surprised me, but it shouldn't have because she had Mexican in her, anyone could see that.

After she paid, she was all set to drive away, but for a stick of gum. She asked if we sell gum, and went inside to buy it. Just think of that, a stick of gum.

"My throat is dry," she said.

She paid for the gum and made a face at the way the

store smelled and the greasy floor. But then she saw my swan sitting on the counter.

"What's this?"

I told her it was a swan.

"Yes, but where did it come from?"

"I carved it."

"You?"

I nodded.

She circled around it. Her eyes were shining. "It's lovely," she said.

I wished the swan had been anywhere but in the greasy gas station store.

"May I?" She ran her fingers down the swan's neck and over the wing. "The likeness is excellent. And it's as if it were ready to take flight." She circled around it again. "Beauty comes easily to you, I can see." She smiled like she had found a prize. Then a serious look passed over her face. "You are an artist," she told me.

"Ah, not really," I said, blushing.

The lady stepped back from the counter to take a full look at the swan. "If you don't mind, I'd like to buy your swan," she said.

I couldn't believe my ears. "Nah," I said, laughing a little.

But the lady didn't want it to slip away, and anyone could see she was someone who got what she wanted.

"My name is Mrs. Linde," she said. "I live over in Santa Rosalia. And I want it for our Arts Pavilion." She looked at me to see if all that was making a difference to me.

"My husband started that pavilion," she said. "He

would be proud to put your swan on display." She told me they were collecting the work of local artists and that she'd pay me a hundred dollars. When I didn't say anything, she must have thought I was refusing her offer. She upped the price again. "I'll pay you two hundred dollars for the swan."

I didn't say anything.

"Are there others?" she asked.

"Not like this," I said. How I carved such a beautiful piece, I wasn't sure, but I didn't tell her that. I didn't tell anybody. For years I sat in my workshop, turning out junk, birds that looked more like trucks and fish that looked like loaves of bread with points on both ends. Then one night I put my head in my hands and prayed to the Blessed Virgin. Look, I told her, if you don't want me to carve, then make this piece turn out like junk, like the rest of them, and I'll stop wasting the wood. But if you do want me to carve, then let me make this piece beautiful and I'll give it to the church in your honor on the Feast of the Assumption.

"This one I kind of promised to the church," I told the lady.

Mrs. Linde pursed her lips. "I see," she said.

Ana

I was in the back shelling peas, and when I heard what Pepillo said I couldn't stand it anymore. I burst through the curtain that separated the small apartment from the gas station. "Three hundred," I told her.

She turned around, surprised. "I thought it wasn't for sale."

I told her she was misinformed. She turned from me to Pepillo, who stood there like a deaf-mute, and then back to me again. She gave me a suspicious look. "Two hundred fifty dollars," she said, and I let her have her way. All that money for one of Pepillo's carvings! How we could use it! And anyone could see it wasn't much to her, this woman in a fancy car with a dark pink dress and high heels.

Where was she going in that outfit?

That Pepillo has no business sense. Telling her it's promised to the church. What possible use could they have for it? And for love or money she wasn't going to be taken back to the shop where she could see all the junk he's done. It's a thing with him. The cars are blowing their horn waiting for him to pump gas, and he's back in the shop, carving his good-for-nothing trinkets. He gives them away, to the doctor, to the grocer, the mayor, but they give us nothing in return.

She turned to Pepillo. "Two hundred fifty dollars, is that alright with you?"

"I am thinking of the church," he said.

"Well, you can always make another one," said the lady in a rushed way. "The church is very patient."

"Of course he can make another one," I told her. "His own wife ought to know."

"Yes," the lady said. She took out two hundred-dollar bills and a fifty from her purse and put them on the counter. "Can you help me to the car with this?" she asked Pepillo.

Pepillo just stood there.

"Go *on*," I hissed at him.

He picked up the swan with the air of a criminal going to the gallows.

When he came back from helping the lady, he still had that hangdog look.

"Now we can pay our bills," I said to try to cheer him up. "Now we can go to the grocer's and hold our heads up high. Is that too much to ask?"

"No," he said lamely. "I guess not."

He didn't dare say what was really on his mind, which was what was he going to tell the saints above because, knowing Pepillo, he probably did some finagling with one of them about the swan.

Everyone knew about Pepillo and his saints. You'd think he was a hustler, the way he was always conning them into this and that. But he'd rather die than double-cross them. If Pepillo wrangled some favor from Saint Peter in exchange for five dollars in the poor box, he'd make good, even if he had to cheat a customer. If he told Saint Francis that he'd feed the squirrels, he'd take the food off his own plate. He walked around in fear of anything to do with the saints. It's as if they had all come to him and said, "We'll make good on our promises but if you even think about welching on your end, we'll know you're going to do it even before you do, and we'll come find you and see that you spend eternity in hell. Understand?"

But to my mind, Pepillo had done nothing wrong. True, the swan was his best carving by far. But now that he had found his way, he could easily carve another one if he really did promise it to the church, and it does sound like the sort of cockamamie thing he would do. That man!

Pepillo stood with a confused look in front of the cash register. He had a week's growth of stubble and a grimy shirt and grease under his fingernails.

"You'd better get shaved," I told him. While he was in the bathroom, I ironed his plaid shirt and white pants. "Go on now, take the money and pay the grocer, before the rich lady changes her mind."

Pepillo

Ana was right. Pay the doctor, the grocer, the butcher, get them all off our backs. I counted the bills carefully and put them into my pocket. How all that money could be so light made me laugh. A man is happy when he hears the jangle of change in his pocket, they say. And twice as happy when the money is all bills.

I started toward town. Past the orange grove, past the old junkyard, over the bridge, I couldn't get what the rich lady said out of my mind. An artist. Me, a grease monkey, a gas pumper, a bum who has to beg credit at every store for a dollar or two. Now an artist. The idea began to hum in my head. An artist. I told the first person I saw, Nelo the bricklayer, going home from work.

"Hey," he said. "I knew it all the time."

"Really?"

"Nah, but it sounds good."

I felt muddled and limp. "Yeah, well, I didn't really do it myself." I tried to set Nelo straight, tell him that I had some help carving the swan.

He started to laugh. "Yeah, you and the communion of saints got together and pulled it off," he said, and laughed harder. Nelo called to his friend, a half a block away. "Hey, Pepillo the artist sold his swan for big bucks!"

"Bravo, Pepillo!"

Soon five or ten people gathered around me shouting, "Bravo!" "We've got to celebrate over a drink."

Before I knew what was happening, a crowd of them hoisted me up on their shoulders and were carrying me toward the bar at the end of town.

Six or seven of them, they carried me through the streets toward the bar, way up high on their shoulders, I held out my hands like wings, like I was skimming through a blue and peaceful sky.

It was almost dinnertime when they set me down at the door to the bar. Ana would be wondering where I was, looking at her watch every two seconds and pacing up and down, trying to decide whether to fry up the onions and the meat or wait for me.

Then it came to me: I'm going to marry that woman. All these years together without a proper wedding. I'm going to the pawnshop tomorrow and buy a ring. Maybe two. Then when she calls herself my wife she won't be lying.

That was the last thought I had before they pushed me through the door to the bar, a ring for my bride.

"Hullo." Nelo waved to the people in the bar. "Drinks all around. On Pepillo!"

Soon there were twenty, thirty people in the bar, all drinking on my money.

They were toasting me. They were toasting themselves. They were toasting swans. "Everyone needs a swan," someone yelled. "They need swans more than they need money rotting in the bank!"

"Yeah, and these swans don't shit!" cried a man with a small moustache and a spiteful look in his eye.

A woman in a pale green dress walked onto the dance floor and began to dance by herself. She did not look at the others, she watched her own hands, which moved gracefully as though they were pushing bubbles up toward the sky.

"Have a beer!" Nicolas the porter at the hotel yelled to me. "It's not every day an artist gets discovered in this rat hole of a town."

"Aah, he doesn't drink anymore," said Nelo, slapping me on the back. "Some promise he made to the saints," he added, rolling his eyes.

"Forget the saints. Everyone drinks tonight!" Nicolas insisted. "Bartender, bring this man a beer. Excuse me, bring this *famous artist* a beer!"

"Come on, Pepillo, even a saint has a drink now and then," cried Nelo.

"Okay, but just one round," I told them, wishing they'd leave me alone. The golden drink was awful, it burned all the way down my throat. Just like I remembered. I sipped it anyway. Then I drank it down.

"Go, Pepillo!" Nicolas shouted. The others were whistling and stamping their feet. "More beer for Pepillo!"

Before I knew it, three beers were sitting in front of me.

With everyone hounding me, what could I do? I had another beer, and another. They tasted great, just like I remembered. Just like old times.

The bartender grabbed my sleeve. "Hey buddy, take a breather," he said.

I felt myself slipping away, down, down the drain until Pepillo wasn't there anymore. Someone else rose up and took over, someone who knew how to have fun, someone who knew what Pepillo had been missing all this time. Someone who knew how to live. An artist.

Was that me betting Ana's gold watch in a poker game?

Was that me ordering the bartender to bring us the best beer in the house?

Was that me standing up every two minutes and shouting, "I am an artist!"

Ana

What luck!

When Pepillo left with the money to pay our bills, I knelt down and made the sign of the cross and thanked the saints for bringing Mrs. Linde our way.

Tomorrow there would be a new me, walking right down to the market and asking the butcher for the good meat. He'd know that we paid our debt, but he wouldn't know that there was even more money in my purse. He would see me open the red wallet and say in an offhand way, "Oh, just let me check my money," and his eyes would open wide at the sight of all those bills! "Yes, señora," he'd say. "A little steak fried with peppers and rice, how good that would taste. Perhaps you'd like some chicken too."

The butcher wouldn't speak mean to me anymore. He would smile when he saw me, he wouldn't make me wait until everyone else had been served and there was no one else at the counter. Not anymore. "Oh yes, señora," he'd say with great respect. "We have just what you like today, the flank steak. For you, the best cut." My dinners would be perfect, like the ones in the magazines. And candles. There would be money for a candle or two. Candle-light brings magic into the house, they say. Everyone in town would hear of my elegant dinners. They would want to know how, they would stop me in the street and ask for the recipes. "Ana," they'd say, "we don't know how you do it." The mayor's wife would come to me when she was having a fancy dinner. "Ana, can you just please help me decide whether to serve the roast chicken or the pork?"

Yes, things will be different now.

The feeling of turning cartwheels overwhelmed me, and right there in our drab little apartment in back of the gas station my body turned over and over with the liveliness of the children in the park.

I walked back to Pepillo's workshop just to be close to the reason for my new life, and a grand idea came into my head: I once heard that all the bars in Ireland had wooden swans. Surely those swans must be old by now. Pepillo could make new swans! All different sizes, in different-color wood. Twenty-five swans at $250 apiece. No, $250 was just to start out. If that rich lady had paid $250, a bar could afford $500.

And Pepillo could carve more, hundreds more. Thousands. Ireland is a big country.

Pepillo could open a factory. A swan factory. Happiness descended on me like a giant billowy white cloud.

Thinking of all those swans made my eyes grow heavy, and I let my head fall onto Pepe's work table, just to close them for a second to get a little rest from all this. A little rest. Soon I was dreaming, of a rose garden with swans bringing me tea and cakes on velvet pillows. Such a beautiful dream I was in, the most beautiful of my life, when the three knocks on the door came. I stayed where I was, my dream was too lovely to abandon. But they were loud, hard knocks that could only mean trouble. At the door, there was a policeman with Pepillo slung over his shoulders, passed out. The policeman came in and dumped Pepillo on the sofa like a deer that had been shot in the heart.

"I'd have thrown him in jail if he hadn't been such a sorry-looking lug," the policeman told me.

Pepillo

Is my head going to explode?

Sometime last night I woke up retching and I've been retching ever since. Kneeling in front of the toilet, with my head in my hands, exhausted from puking, I called to Ana. "I think I'm going to die."

"Dying would be too good for you," she shouted back from somewhere in the apartment. Why did she have to be so unsympathetic when even she could hear that my Maker was calling me?

I sank into a heap on the floor. At least the tile made me feel cool. Where was the Pepillo of last night, the one who knew how to live? My own cursed self was back, and it had come back dumber and more miserable than before.

My head throbbed and my whole body felt shaken and weak as if the gasoline pump had been used on me.

"Get your poor excuse for a self up off the floor and get to work," Ana yelled to me.

What a cold heart she had!

Only with the greatest effort did I pull myself up and stagger out to the rusty chair in the shade, waiting for a car to come by for gas.

Before long, Mrs. Jacinto, the pharmacist's wife, rode up on her bicycle. She wheeled it over toward the air machine.

"We're not giving away free air anymore," I called to her weakly.

She paid no attention to me.

Ana flagged her down. "Take a look at what the cat dragged in," Ana said to her, nodding at me.

Mrs. Jacinto came up to me and squinted. She was a fat woman with the smell of garlic always about her. Sweat ran down her forehead and neck from riding her bicycle on the hottest day of the year. Unbuttoning the top two buttons of her dress and fanning herself with her other hand, she scowled at me.

"Open your mouth," she said with the same disgusted tone in which Ana spoke to me. "Stick out your tongue." Then she put her index finger on my cheekbone and pulled my skin down so as to see straight into my lower eyelids.

"You've done quite a job on yourself," she announced. "But you'll live, unfortunately." She took a lemon out of her bag and cut it in half. "Now put one under each arm and sit in a dark room and wait for your health to return."

She stepped away to speak with Ana. I tried to follow their conversation, but they turned their backs and began to whisper, looking like conspirators in a plot to do away with me.

One of the lemon halves fell from under my arm. Like she had eyes in the back of her head, Mrs. Jacinto whirled around and shouted at me, "Now you listen to me, mister. This is the best remedy you can have for what ails you, and you'd better do as I say. Put that lemon back under your arm!" She returned to her huddle with Ana.

I sat there wishing to Saint Jude she would melt into a puddle on the ground.

Finally, she got back on her bike.

As she was leaving, Mrs. Jacinto turned toward me and shook her finger. "And swear to the Holy Mother of God that you will never set foot in a barroom again!"

Ana

If there's one thing that makes me crazy, it's people sleeping in the middle of the day. It's not right, it's not natural, it's a sign of the worst kind of idleness.

Right after Mrs. Jacinto left, Pepillo went to the bedroom and fell asleep with the shades pulled down and the window shut.

It was suffocating in there.

Finally I couldn't stand it. I went in and pulled the covers off him and shouted right in his ear. "Did you pay the bills?"

When he hid his head under the pillow, I asked louder, "Did you pay the bills?"

He just lay there like a weasel.

"Where's the money then?"

Pepillo grabbed his head and moaned.

"You spent it," I accused him.

He moaned louder.

"All of it?" My voice was rising to a dangerous point.

He turned over facedown on the bed.

I was shrieking now. "You spent two hundred fifty dollars buying drinks for those lowlifes and playing cards!"

A sound came up. A muffled moan.

"What?!" I screamed at him.

The same sound.

It sounded like he was saying *more*.

"MORE? What more?" I shouted.

Pepillo turned over and sat up on the bed. His shoulders were shaking. In disgust, I realized he was crying.

"I had to leave an IOU from the gas station receipts." He was bawling like a baby. "A hundred dollars."

A string of curses flew out of my mouth, the curses my mother taught me that were so bad even *she* didn't know what they meant. An old magazine was lying on the floor by the bed, and I rolled it up as if I was going to swat a fly. Like a madwoman I began hitting Pepillo about the head and the neck and the shoulders and then all over, wherever I could find to strike until I fell down on the floor, sobbing like a baby myself.

Ana

I thought we had seen the worst of this, but no. The very next day the silver car pulled up in the gas station again. It had a serious, disapproving look to it, like the bearer of bad news. I have a sixth sense about these matters. The rich lady wasn't here for gas, that I knew immediately, so I wasn't surprised when she didn't stop at the pump, but pulled up right outside the little office. I was afraid that she had heard about Pepillo's night and didn't want to be associated with a shiftless drunk. I feared the worst, especially when I saw her get something out of the backseat of the car.

Not knowing what else to do, I opened the cash register and pretended to count up the coins so I wouldn't see her when she walked in.

As if that made any difference to her.

"Hello," she said. "Is your husband here?" She was wearing a dress with small blue flowers and the swan was in her arms, which strained under its weight.

"He's not feeling well," I said, not adding that Pepillo might never feel well again. All day and all night he slept, getting up only to retch until nothing remained inside him, not even himself. This morning he went shirtless, still refusing any nourishment but sugar water, still refusing to listen to anything I said. Covering his ears with his hands, he went outside and sat on the ground like the most disappointed man in the world. He has been this way since nine o'clock this morning.

"Oh, well I must see him. It won't take long at all."

I regarded her in silence for a moment. Her expression was more serious than the other day. Her mouth remained closed and there was a heaviness about her, a sense that she was doing something she was not enjoying. Maybe she noticed a defect, that's all I could imagine, and I asked her if there was something the matter with the swan.

"Oh, no," she said. "It's beautiful."

I began to be relieved. Maybe she wanted more swans and she was bringing it to show Pepillo just what she liked. For the first time in more than a day, a glimmer of hope was mine. "Would you like some gum?" I asked her, suddenly feeling extraordinarily grateful to her. "Some coffee?"

"No thank you." She gave a little smile that was both polite and impatient. "I would just like to see your husband."

"My husband is around back," I told her, upset that she would find him in such a pathetic state. I stole a glance out the window, hoping that he had somehow pulled himself together. But no, there he was looking like a bum. His pants were ripped in four places and he was shirtless. On his head was an old straw hat of mine with a tired red rose on the front. He was lying on the scrubby ground under that old weed tree by the garbage, and the flies were buzzing. I could smell the garbage from here.

Pepillo

Only the old mesquite tree was my friend that day, giving me shade and a place to lean and not scolding me. For a few moments I was peaceful there, lying down with the lemon halves still under my arms. I was dreaming of flying over a blue lagoon with not a human in sight, only the green of the trees and the raw salty smell of the water.

A noise startled me.

I opened my eyes to the sight of Mrs. Linde. It made me jump out of my skin.

"Hello," she said. "I hope I'm not disturbing you."

I rose up on my elbows. "No, not at all."

"What happened to you?" she said.

"Oh, nothing," I answered, probably too quickly.

She stared at me for a minute like she was concerned. But she got over it. "I'm returning your swan," she said, just like that.

I thought I hadn't heard correctly, so I asked her to repeat it. The second time she said it, it felt like a vat of molasses falling on me, trapping me in a dark, sticky mess that I might never be free of.

I asked her why she was bringing the swan back.

She thought for a minute. "It's not right. It's for the church, as you said."

"Don't worry about that. It's fine," I stammered.

"No, it's not," she insisted. "You didn't want to sell it to me in the first place. Your instinct was better than mine." She put the swan on the ground beside me. "I don't like to interfere in God's business. So I'll leave you your swan. And you give me back the money. Simple as that."

Not for the world could I let that happen.

I began to stutter. "W-w-well . . . don't you want the swan? You said you thought it was wonderful."

"That it is, señor," she said. "No one can take that away from you."

The panic that swept through me came out in a rush of words. "Look, the workmanship on him, the feathers on the wings, as lifelike as you'll ever see." My mind was barely a step ahead of my mouth. "And the beak, you'll never see another like it. This swan is carved out of tupelo. You can see the grain. I might not ever come by another chunk of tupelo like that."

"No," she said with the indifferent look of the rich. "You may not."

What I said next, I cannot remember, the way I jabbered on, giving her one, ten, a hundred reasons why she must keep the swan. All the while, she gazed at me with the uncon-cerned look of someone watching cars passing in the street.

Then she said the thing I dreaded most. "I'll take the money now."

I was too petrified to utter a word.

"Ah," she said. "It's gone already."

I admitted that it was.

"Oh, señor," she said, and let out a low whistle. "Well, then you'll have to pay me off week by week," she said. She shook her head and gave a little laugh.

That laugh. Not a guffaw, or a giggle. Just a stupid little I-should-have-known-it laugh.

I felt like I was running up a slippery hill and couldn't

get my footing. "I can make you another, just like it," I begged her.

She frowned. "You can try, but it's unlikely that another swan will be the same as the first."

"You'll see, it'll be exactly the same. You'll see!" I cried, watching her turn her back on me and walk away.

As soon as she said it, I knew she was right. I didn't have it in me, that much I was sure of. Two weeks went by and I didn't even try to carve another swan, or anything else. After a month I packed up my carving knives and sandpaper and blocks of wood and put them in a crate. The next week I made a present of all my carving things to Nelo, just to show no hard feelings.

All that was so long ago it seems like a dream. I am a different man now. These days I sell tires and car parts from my old workshop, and people are always asking to borrow money from me. Ana would love me now, but shortly after Mrs. Linde returned the swan, Ana ran off with the driver of a truck full of cauliflowers headed for Atlanta.

Right after that I brought the swan down to Father Cabrero at the church; they displayed it on the altar until there were so many summer flowers that there wasn't really room for it. The swan wound up at the old people's home down the road where the men in wheelchairs had a grand time tossing rubber rings around its neck. Now I suppose it's in the back of a closet somewhere.

It's funny how things end up. Not too long after that business with the swan, I heard the Arts Pavilion in Santa Rosalia closed up. People weren't interested in culture, someone said. Ever since, the ground level has been a donut shop, which is very popular. As for Mrs. Linde, she's had her problems too. I finally sent her a check for the money I owed her, but she never cashed it. A few years back I heard she spent a lot of time in the hospital watching her husband die.

Every now and then I say a prayer to the Blessed Virgin for him.

11
As Told by Rosalba Vilar
1982

It began that Wednesday morning in May, and what a morning it was, so bright and full of promise. It invited us to dream. All the ladies of the Altar Guild of the Church of San Lorenzo felt it, even the Host tasted sweeter on our tongues, and we came together after eight o'clock Mass and in a wave floated over to Mercedes Comche's old shop to have our coffee. Our hearts were full, and to each of us they whispered that it was time to make a bigger mark in the world of the spirit than just arranging the altar flowers and laundering the sacristy linens.

We were all speaking at once and from our chatter rose an idea to reopen the old Mission Chapel that had been built by the Oblates of Mary and boarded up since the last century.

Yes, but how? What a pack of silly old geese we were, we knew that, and agreed we must have a leader, someone stronger and more merciless than we were, someone who could keep us from wandering off, someone who would show us the most direct path to our vision. The name of

Ayela Linde was mentioned, and it caused a stiff silence from others in the group.

"Well," said Hortensia Drenk as she put down her coffee cup. "We used to be very friendly. But she's changed," Horty added and, crossing her arms over her chest and lowering her voice, she complained that Ayela Linde rarely worshipped in the parish ever since her boys were grown and off on their own, she drove all the way to the tumbledown church in Oderada. All that way to sit in the back pews with the Mexican day laborers. Hortensia shook her head. "Now what is the meaning of that?"

I laughed to myself because I remember Ayela once telling me that she preferred the company of the poor in church. "They have only one reason to go," she said.

Beatriz Delgado sat up in her chair. "Well, if she's so taken by run-down churches, then this is just the thing for her. She will be the one to lead us." On her wedding day thirty-five years ago, Beatriz Delgado had looked like an angel in an ecru lace gown with her hair curled and massed on top of her head, and because I have never seen her look so beautiful either before or since I have a hard time trusting her.

Beatriz Delgado didn't like Ayela Linde. She didn't like how Ayela had risen into the town's high society from a poor birth and an improper upbringing. She disliked even more Ayela's refusal to become one of us in the Altar Guild. "I'm not a joiner," Ayela Linde made a point of saying, and so, you see, how she brings things on herself.

At times I, too, think that Ayela Linde has a stingy heart. But what do we really know about anyone? What

Ayela Linde did in the matter of the Mission Chapel surprised even me, but on occasion we all do things that are unlike ourselves or so like our own selves, it's hard to tell the difference.

The ladies of the Altar Guild began to suggest others to lead us.

But Beatriz Delgado was a dog with a bone. "Ayela Linde will lead us in this, and I'll ask her myself," she told us. "Horty, since you were such a good friend of hers, you'll come along with me."

In their high heels and matching handbags, Hortensia Drenk and Beatriz Delgado went to see Ayela Linde on a Tuesday morning in June, and gave us all a full account. They were greeted at the door by the housekeeper, Concha, who showed them around back, where they found Ayela Linde on her knees digging in the garden.

She was pruning the old roses, which she liked to do, and for which she had a flair. When they were sturdy enough, she often took them down to the roadsides in the open country and returned them to where they belonged. People said that it was because she wanted to spread something of herself over the whole land, but I don't think it was that. "These roses are the only things that have never given me a moment's trouble," she often told me. "And they're too lovely to keep to myself."

Hortensia Drenk went over to where Ayela Linde was kneeling in front of the rosebushes and put the Altar Guild's request right to her.

"We want you to lead us in a project to reopen the old Mission Chapel," she said.

Ayela laid down her garden trowel and sat back on her haunches. "I wouldn't have the slightest idea of what to do," she replied.

"You're too modest," said Beatriz Delgado in a curt way.

In a singsong voice as if she were addressing schoolchildren, Hortensia spoke about the simple beauty of the old Mission Chapel and what a shame it was to keep it locked away from the people of Santa Rosalia and the world beyond.

Both Hortensia and Beatriz swore that Ayela Linde had actually breathed in their request and let it spiral around and sink deep into her and for a brief moment seriously considered it, but in the end it came hurtling back out in the exhaust of her sigh. "I can't help you," she said without apologizing.

Still, they came away awed by her decisiveness, and thinking that though Ayela had refused their request, she could be useful in some way to them. That's when they turned to me. They seemed to think that being an old and close friend, I could persuade her to join our cause. Though we may have both been born on Violeta Street and Ayela Linde still came down there to sit on my patio and take a glass of lemonade every now and then, we were not close. I don't know if anyone was close to Ayela Linde, except perhaps her husband, Frederick, who had saved her from herself, but that is not the same thing as being close.

Reluctantly, I agreed to go, and Hortensia Drenk and Beatriz Delgado took me along on their next visit to urge Ayela Linde to join the cause of the Mission Chapel. Ayela Linde's house was one of the town's old Spanish-style places, so well cared for that it appeared like a jewel box, as if you could open it up and find the most precious objects inside. I didn't go there often, but when I did the sight of it took me by the throat with its loveliness and made me bow my head in gratitude that someone from Violeta Street had been chosen to inhabit it. Particularly because of all the small gray houses on Violeta Street, the house where Ayela lived with her mother and her grandmother was the smallest and grayest. Inside was in disarray, the disarray of women without men. The furniture wore leftover fabrics from Felidia Garzón's dress shop. The sofa wore turquoise, the windows wore drapes of yellow and green flowers, the chairs were wrapped in a silky pink cloth. Everywhere were boxes of colored foil, stacks of materials, baskets of thread and buttons and trims. The smell was that of old face powder or too-ripe flowers, a smell that would stifle a man. But none of them cared about that. "No man has stepped across this threshold since they carried my papa out in a coffin twenty years ago," Felidia Garzón had been proud of saying. And everybody in Santa Rosalia knew that Felidia Garzón had barely laid eyes on Ayela's father: people said that he came and went in the same night so fast that it left an undying chill in the heart of the child he never knew he had.

After knowing Ayela Garzón in those circumstances, her present house always startled me with its good sense and pleasant air.

Ayela was in the parlor with the grand piano and that painting of the waves at Veracruz. She was eating the same breakfast she had eaten since we were girls, café con leche and a cruller, and a slice of melon, which she put down and with an annoyed expression, listened to our request for a donation to the resurrection of the Mission Chapel.

"You're confusing me with my husband," said Ayela Linde. "I don't have a penny to my name." Hortensia Drenk nudged me to step up and speak, but before the words formed in my mind, Ayela snapped, "And you above all people, Rosalba, should understand that."

Her words stung me and I stepped back, unsure of what she meant. It wasn't until a week later I recalled that in the first days of their marriage, Ayela Linde had vowed that she would never use anything of her husband's for her gain, neither his money or his name, though I had dismissed it at the time as girlish pride. Some people said Ayela was a gold digger for marrying Frederick Linde when he came striding into town more than forty years ago, but Ayela never cared anything for money, she was scornful of it in the way that those who have it can be, and those who never will. Still, she might have relented a bit for the Mission Chapel, I thought.

After that second meeting, the ladies of the Altar Guild were disgusted with Ayela Linde and her quarrelsome ways. Several meetings were spent disapproving of her spirit and planning snubs on the street, and the lot of us agreed not to attend the reception that she and her husband were giving for a visiting musician from Mérida.

Finally the Altar Guild lost interest in her and seized upon the mayor's wife, Estrella Denud, to lead us in resurrecting the Mission Chapel. Estrella Denud was a thin woman with a severe air, and she rose to the task like a martinet, clipboard in hand and with the added advantage of putting the buzz in the mayor's ear about siphoning some funds from the general treasury for our undertaking.

From her husband the mayor, Estrella Denud had learned the value of public ceremony. Like clockwork at half past ten on the morning of September 15, the drum roll sounded and the small crowd, consisting mostly of the ladies of the Altar Guild, stood at attention in front of the Mission Chapel, which, with its sagging roof and broken windows, looked more pitiful than we had remembered. When Estrella gave the signal, the mayor broke the lock on the doors, and the presence of God, which had been bottled up for decades, rushed out. We were surprised by the violent mustiness of it, as if left to himself God had taken on the same mortal odor as a world full of rummage-sale clothes. Even Father Anthony Maria fanned himself with his breviary to chase away the smell.

Estrella Denud would not be stopped. "Well," she said, walking briskly into the interior of the chapel. "God should be happy today. Daylight has come into his house."

We followed her inside. A few birds were startled from their nests by our voices, and flew up and out. For some reason, the fluttering caused Hortensia Drenk to shriek, "Rats!" She quickly covered her mouth and looked embarrassed to have raised her voice in a holy place. Hortensia's panic upset all of us, and one of the older ladies of the Altar Guild nearly fainted and had to be taken outside by the mayor himself.

To be sure, the chapel was in shambles, but the floor was by far the worst sight. There were brown stains from the leaking roof and thick splotches of droppings from the generations of winged and four-legged creatures that had found shelter in the neglected chapel.

Estrella Denud dismissed our sour looks and whispered laments about the droppings. "Those animals are God's creatures too," she said and brushed past us on her way to inspect the altar.

The ladies of the Altar Guild retreated outside to wait for her. Fifteen minutes later, Estrella emerged from the chapel and paused to write a few notes on her clipboard. With the voice of authority, she announced that volunteers would be needed to spruce up the place. "If we at least clean out the filth, people will see a worthwhile project and the money will come streaming in for bigger repairs," she said, in the same breath declaring that the Mission Chapel would throw open its doors to the waiting congregation just four weeks later on the Feast of the Rosary in October.

Instead of the applause she expected, Estrella saw only the exchange of worried glances among the members of the Altar Guild. She let it be known that our lack of enthusiasm would not do and reprimanded us severely. "Now we'll see the extent of your devotion, ladies."

Beatriz Delgado had tears in her eyes, and reflected the defeat we all felt in our hearts at the impossibility of the task that lay before us. To a woman, we were sorry that we had ever heard of the Mission Chapel.

Only Hortensia Drenk came forward. She went up to Estrella Denud and looked her coldly in the eye. "This is men's work!" she exclaimed.

"Whatever you say, but it's got to be done," Estrella replied.

We took Hortensia Drenk at her word, which we thought was inspired, and in the coming weeks, several of the ladies lent their handymen to do the dirty work of clearing the filth from the church.

The work went on all day, every day. While the men worked inside, we ladies remained on the steps of the chapel, rosaries in hand, praying to the Blessed Virgin for the souls of the handymen who had rescued us from such a distasteful task. At noon, one of us ran up to Mercedes Comche's to bring buckets of fried meat and rice for their noonday meal.

Thursday of the second week was my day to fetch the lunch.

While the men ate under the trees, I went inside to see how the cleaning was progressing.

One worker, I noticed, had stayed behind, and was still on his knees, scrubbing with a white root. It was the root that stopped me, the same root that had been used long ago in the homes of the poor. My grandmother had used it, my mother too, she had taught me to dip it in the clear water and wring it out so it brought forth an ocean of suds. I hadn't seen one since I was a child.

The sight of that root drew me toward the worker, and I sat in the pew just in back of him. He was wearing workman's clothes and a cap and I couldn't see his face. I was struck by the root, of course, but also by the way the scrubber seemed to enjoy the scrubbing, as though he was absorbed in kind of trance.

After a time, the figure looked up from his work, perhaps because he felt the weight of my gaze.

I thought I might faint, because it was Ayela Linde.

"It's what I know how to do," she said matter-of-factly.

A strange confusion began to overtake me. Was this more

of her ancient arrogance or a humble new turn of cheek? Did she want to be found out in her remarkable deed, or simply make her contribution quietly, away from the greedy eyes of the Altar Guild?

I couldn't put a name on what she was doing here, and was at a loss as to how to feel.

In my bewilderment, she looked at me as if perhaps she had once known me in another lifetime, but in the end didn't care.

I was about to say something, at least offer her some lunch, but before I could speak, Ayela dropped her eyes and continued her scrubbing.

I passed by her without a word.

Whether it was selfish of me I could never really determine, but I said nothing of that incident to anyone. And no one else in the town of Santa Rosalia ever knew the lengths to which Ayela Linde had gone in the matter of the Mission Chapel.

12
Victim
1987

Can't they see what a bad business this is?

It's more Father's doing than Mother's. He's always at it, trying to make things right. She goes along, but knows it isn't worth the trouble.

From upstairs I heard them come in the front door, Father and the victim. The guy whose house was just trashed in the hurricane, whose wife died when a tree fell through the roof and crushed her.

What a wreck, all those towns down toward the river, the poor towns. Funny, how it's always the poor towns that get it. Father is undone, he hates to see the suffering. So of all ways to help, what does he do? Father drives right over to the shelter in Olaca and picks out someone on whom to bestow the Linde castoffs.

"Welcome, Mr. Varne, come right in," I heard my father say in his jovial one-of-the-guys way. Without having even seen him before he drove off, I knew my father was wearing his khakis and a catalog shirt to give him that casual, not too rich look. Though he means well, Father doesn't understand that his way of comforting another human being only makes that person excruciatingly uncomfortable.

Father brought the poor guy in, sat him down in the parlor. "We'll just wait for Mrs. Linde and we'll go down to the basement. See if there's anything you can use there," Father said, and launched into his barrage of small talk.

I could just see it, Father unable to sit still, walking up and down, going on about which vegetables were in season in his obsequious way, the foolproof topic of the weather off-limits to him for obvious reasons.

Mr. Varne must be squirming in his seat. What does he care about the flavor of heirloom tomatoes grown without pesticides?

Even from up here in the bedroom of my boyhood I could feel Mr. Varne's discomfort as he sank into the chair and tried for the life of him to figure what this was all about. Why Father drove down to the emergency shelter in Olaca in his big gunboat of a Cadillac and brought him here for handouts. Will there be money for him here too, and how much, is surely on Mr. Varne's mind, and there will be that, later, much later, maybe not even tonight. That must be the point, right? Puzzle as he might, Mr. Varne can only come up with this, the money. Even he can see we have it, with all these shining wood floors and oil paintings and velvet furniture.

Maybe Mr. Varne wasn't interested in money. But he was asked to come here, singled out from hundreds of others less fortunate, there must be something in that. Whatever Mr. Varne was thinking, he was doing his best to rise to the occasion. I could feel him repaying his host at every moment, nodding his head regularly at my father's good-natured monologue that had turned to the hopeless state of the local newspapers. He laughed when my father laughed, clearing his throat, brightening his eyes.

I cringed in shame.

"Jesse, let's go down now, we don't want to keep them waiting," Gigi cooed, floating out of the bathroom dressed for a nightclub in a low-cut black dress with sequins around the bosom. She kissed me on the cheek, I pulled her on my lap, and she giggled. Then the guilt came rushing in. How could I be doing something like that when downstairs Mr. Varne will never again be able to see his wife float out of the bathroom smelling like a department-store perfume counter, never be able to pull her on to his lap and bury his head in her bosom and shut out the world?

"In a minute, sweet pea," I said, putting off the moment when we would have to join our guest.

"Alright, lovey," she said. "I'll just fix my hair then."

That's my third wife for you. Agreeable. Hair as platinum as Marilyn's. And happy. The other two were drags. They started out happy enough, but then that Mother thing took over. Where were you, Jesse? You were supposed to be home an hour ago! Did you fix the sink? Are the bills paid? You said you'd be home at seven . . .

Not Gigi.

She was a ticket taker at the air show I was flying in. We got married in Vegas last week. Stayed for a two-week honeymoon and flew right down to meet the folks.

The reaction was underwhelming.

Mother sighed. "Do you have to marry them all?

Haven't you heard of dating, Jesse?" she said to me as soon as she could get me alone.

Father calls Gigi Loretta, number two's name. Now that she's gone, Father misses Loretta. She was a night clerk at the Lemon Tree Inn in New Orleans before she met me, and used to bring him coffee from Café du Monde. That gave Father something to go on about, thinking that it was some common ground they shared, the coffee, the beignets, the French Quarter. Though it is probably just a case of the lesser of two evils, Loretta or the black-sequined Gigi.

Poor Father. The less fortunate make him uncomfortable with his own health and wealth and brains, which, unless everyone else can have them too, he doesn't really want. Maybe he's even ashamed of himself for being so. He should have been born paraplegic and homeless, that would have made him happy.

I had to smile at my own insight.

"Alright, Gigi. We're on," I finally succumbed. "Let's get this over with."

"Oh, goody." Gigi dropped her brush and stood right up. "I love a party."

When I reminded her of the circumstances of our guest and the purpose of this get-together, she put her arms around my neck. "Well, then he needs some fun more than any of us," she said in all seriousness.

On the stairs, Gigi let out a little shriek. "Oh my God. I've got a run!" She scurried back up to change her stockings. Without Gigi by my side, my nerve left me, and I tiptoed the rest of the way down the stairs and made a beeline for the kitchen.

Too late.

"Jesse, come meet Mr. Varne." Father waved me over.

"Hello," I called sheepishly.

Then Mr. Varne did something insane. He stood up when I came in the room. It made me cringe again. Then the thought hit me that perhaps I had misinterpreted Mr. Varne's rising, that it was not a sign of respect for me, and really, why should he have any, but a sudden urge to stretch his feet or a bad wedgie. Because of my quandary, I didn't tell him to sit.

Father remarked to Mr. Varne that I had just gotten married, though naturally he left out the detail about the third time.

Mr. Varne was a large man, half a head taller than Father, his teeth were shockingly white, his skin butterscotch and unlined. Anyone could see he had been through hell. There was a profound fatigue about him, as though he wore lead weights under his clothes. At the news of my recent marriage, he managed a smile, and, looking genuinely happy for me, he reached to shake my hand. "Congratulations."

I muttered my thanks, trying to avoid his eyes.

Mr. Varne was dressed in a Dallas Cowboys T-shirt and faded too-tight, too-short jeans that were no doubt made available to him at the shelter. He had a three- or four-day stubble and looked to be in his fifties, about ten years older than I was, which had the effect of making his indignity all the greater. Older and down and out was tough to take, and I was seized with the feeling that I must make this pitiful afternoon bearable for him.

"Well, I think Concha's got up some special chicken for

us," I stammered, seizing on the first thing I could think of to keep Mr. Varne's mind from wandering back to the recent loss of his wife. "She does this Tex-Mex thing with it. It's been a favorite ever since I was a boy," I said, my own unnaturally enthusiastic voice sickening me.

Mr. Varne regarded me with uncomprehending eyes, then muttered an "oh" and looked embarrassed. I wanted to kick myself, making a reference to a cook when Mr. Varne has never had a cook, unless it was his wife, and there we were at that subject again.

Father didn't miss a beat. "I could eat chicken ten times a day," he said and began to talk about the various breeds of chicken that local farmers were raising. "Did you ever raise chickens, Mr. Varne?"

"No, I did not," Mr. Varne replied.

Before the stupidity of Father's chicken-raising question fully penetrated my brain, I noticed a glimmer of a smile from Mr. Varne as he looked beyond us out into the hall.

"Heeelllooo," Gigi said, striding in, her hand outstretched. "Charmed, I'm sure, Mr. Varne."

Father winced. "Loretta," he said with an awkward laugh. "We're going to be digging around the basement." He gestured toward her outfit. "You'll get that dress dirty."

Gigi swished by him as though he wasn't speaking to her. That's my girl!

Mr. Varne, who hadn't taken his seat since I came in, took Gigi's hand and kissed it. "Charmed," he repeated. This bit of chivalry from Mr. Varne surprised me. I would not have taken him for the gallant type, despite the burden of his recent loss. My wife was beaming at him, and I wanted to throw my arms around her, the least likely one here to be able to comfort Mr. Varne, yet perhaps he sensed something in her beyond her obvious attributes, a common have-not to the Lindes' collective have.

Mr. Varne congratulated Gigi on her marriage.

"Oh, thank you." Gigi giggled. "We drove right up to Vegas after the air show. That's where we met." She giggled again. "My husband's a pilot, you know," she said, gazing adoringly at me.

"A pilot," Mr. Varner repeated.

"Oh, just an air-show pilot," I said. "You know, acrobatics in a plane, loops, rolls, spins, tailslides." I flip-flopped my hand in the air like it was a plane doing backflips.

"That's just what he did in the show," Gigi said proudly.

"He could have been a commercial pilot, but it wasn't for him," said Father, proceeding to bore Mr. Varne with his usual shtick about my inability to toe the line in the world of business and practicality.

Just then, Mother joined us. "So glad you could come, Mr. Varne," she said in a businesslike manner and, without waiting for a response, started off toward the basement. "Let's go see what we can find for you." We trailed behind her down the narrow stairs to the basement where our past had been stashed. Father brought up the rear, with Gigi regaling a passive Mr. Varne about the slot machines in Vegas.

The basement was rather small as basements go, dark and musty, with the washer/dryer in the corner next to a big metal double sink. An oversized freezer stood on the far wall, and to the right a door led to boxes and boxes of Linde castoffs.

"Well, now, Mr. Varne, I suppose you need everything," Mother said matter-of-factly. I could have killed her for putting it so baldly.

Mr. Varne chuckled softly. "I sure do, ma'am."

That was signal for the Lindes to send Mr. Varne into his post-hurricane life armed with more useless objects than he could have ever imagined. The only good thing was that in the work at hand, which Mother took by the horns, Father stopped his relentless patter, and seemed to relegate himself to skulk around the shadows of this new activity.

As far as the boxes were concerned, Mother seemed to have X-ray vision. "Let's put aside whatever you think you can use, Mr. Varne," she said and unpacked some old china and silverware, pots and pans, and all manner of kitchen utensils.

"An omelet pan is always a good thing to have," she said, brandishing a copper-bottomed pan that no one in this household ever used.

"Yes, ma'am," said Mr. Varne, trying to be pleasant, despite the fact that he had probably never cooked an omelet in his life. He looked away, maybe recalling the food he used to eat for dinner with his wife in their small brightly lit kitchen in the four-room house in Olaca, the TV droning on in the background, the meal maybe just some beans or eggs or sausage, but it had the certain flavor he had eaten for thirty years, the food tasting of the particular oil his wife used to cook with, and the amount of salt and spices, and the enthusiasm or reluctance with which she put the food on the table; you grow to love a taste like that even if you don't like it.

"We'll hold these for you until you get your new quarters," Mother said, like Mr. Varne's new "quarters" were going to be some grand place instead of a broken-down trailer, and that's if he was lucky.

Concha came down with some sandwiches and drinks, which she put on a board that Father had laid across the double sink.

"Concha, did you bring some of that famous Tex-Mex chicken of yours?"

"No," she snapped at me. "You boys never liked it so I stopped making it." I blushed, embarrassed to be scolded and caught in a lie in front of Mr. Varne, though my transgressions went unnoticed by our guest, who was in the thrall of a sandwich iron Mother had presented for his consideration.

"How about a beer, Mr. Varne?" asked Father.

Mr. Varne looked up, surprised. "I don't drink, sir," he replied and returned to examining the sandwich iron.

His innocent refusal of a drink made me feel more ashamed of myself and I declined a beer as well, although God knew I could have used one. But if a man who lost everything could go it alone, well then so could I. After I had made such a point of turning down the beer, watching the others lift their glasses to let the booze do its trick, I began to feel a hint of resentment toward the good Mr. Varne, even if it was only beer. Was he a better man than I because he didn't drink? Because he had lost home and wife? Because the impersonal vengeance of weather had chosen to cut its vicious path through the life of Mr. Varne and not mine? A tightness came over me, and I could feel my lips narrow in irritation as I bit into a sandwich.

I glared at Mr. Varne, kneeling there like a dog digging through yesterday's garbage, mumbling something under his breath to himself. The idea that he was probably saying a prayer of thanks for our largesse exasperated me all the more.

Gigi sensed something had upset me and reached for my hand. A feeling of bitterness toward the great Mr. Varne made me take Gigi's hand and bring it to my lips. I looked pointedly at Mr. Varne to gauge the effect it was having on him, but he remained unaware of my little stab at his heart, trying to decide whether a pair of Xavier's cast-off dungarees might fit him.

Mother began to shift through a box that contained clothes we had worn as kids. "Do you have children, Mr. Varne?" my mother asked.

"No," he answered from across the room. "We never did," he said, with a little surprise that that was the case.

"Oh, I love children," Gigi said. "Jesse and I are going to have six."

No one said anything.

Father looked away, disapproving of Gigi's bad taste in discussing a private matter in public, or dreading the thought of Gigi as the mother of his grandchildren.

Mother hadn't heard, or pretended she hadn't.

"Don't you think Gigi would make a great mother?" I said jovially, though my real intention was to stick it to Father, who had made no secret of his less than warm feelings about my dear third wife.

Father didn't respond. His face registered the weight of being trapped in his own hypocrisy. After all, we had been taught to embrace all people as our equals and our companions on the planet. Just not marry them. Glumly, he helped himself to another sandwich.

Mr. Varne registered a look of understanding at the lack of response from both Mother and Father. He glanced up, eyes widening like an animal sensing something out of place. It wasn't a big motion, but I saw it, I was on the lookout for reactions to my statement about Gigi and it tickled me no end that Mr. Varne had put himself in my camp.

Mother opened a garment bag of Father's old suits. "What line of work are you in, Mr. Varne?" she asked.

"I'm a mason, ma'am."

"Well then, you and Frederick look to be about the same size. How about one of these?" I couldn't believe my ears. Mr. Varne was taller and bigger-boned than Father. And hadn't he just told her he was a mason? And she supposed he was going to wear a suit to work?

Mr. Varne rose and went to look over the suits. "I sing in the choir at church," he said. "This one might do," he said, picking up one of Father's signature cream-colored suits that he was sure to pop out of if he could get it on in the first place.

"Oh, Mr. Varne, that is so nice!" Gigi cooed. "I used to sing in the choir too. Do you do this one?" She started a round of some unrecognizable thing about Mary the Flower, belting it out clear and strong, though sadly off-key.

Father turned away to have another beer. Mother said nothing. Only Mr. Varne showed her some kindness. "Yes," he said. "Yes, we do sing that."

Mother renewed the charge. "Look here, Mr. Varne, a sewing basket, and a gilt-framed mirror, and an old Santa Fe blanket." Mother held up item after item. She was indefatigable in the ideas she had for Mr. Varne's new life. She unearthed a statue of a bare-breasted, armless goddess. "Mr.

Varne, I always loved this piece. It's Diana, no Vesta. Vesta, goddess of hearth and home. Why that's perfect. Won't you take it? We just have no room for it anymore."

"Ayela, do you think that's really practical?" Father chimed in. I had to agree: just what Mr. Varne needed for his trailer, a fifty-pound armless statue of no possible meaning to him.

Mr. Varne looked helplessly from Mother to Father, not knowing which one to side with, a predicament in which I've often found myself.

Mother was adamant about her statue. "Unless you have no objection, Mr. Varne, I'll put it aside for you."

"Yes, ma'am," replied Mr. Varne, teaming up with the stronger opponent.

Mother stood on tiptoes to pull down a box from the top shelf. "Christmas decorations, Mr. Varne. You're going to need them. A few strings of lights, old glass ornaments, and, look at this, an eight-pointed star for the top of the tree."

That did it. Mr. Varne was knocked off balance by the soppy sentimental decorations. To have to cook an omelet by himself or a grilled cheese sandwich was one thing, but to have to go it alone at that loneliest of family holidays was too much for him to consider. He didn't respond to Mother, but fell back from his knees to sit cross-legged on the floor, shoulders hunched, staring off. The specter of Mr. Varne alone in front of his Christmas tree decorated with Linde hand-me-downs cast a pall over our little band of do-gooders.

I spotted a cigarette lighter in the form of a jet plane that my brother Xavier had given to me when I began flight school. "Look, Mr. Varne, you can't be without this," I said in a friendly way, desperate to take us all beyond the Christmas decorations. Just to make sure we didn't bog down in the lights and ornaments, I set out on a monologue, the subject of which was pilots. I explained about the different types of pilots, jet pilots and agricultural pilots and photogrammetry pilots, I talked about the required training for each and the salaries they might expect, and the instruments they flew by. I did not skimp on the technical terms, the nuances of plotting, air navigation, instrument rules. Minutes passed and I was still holding forth. Oh, I could be boring.

All the while I was rambling on, I kept watch over Mr. Varne. But it was inevitable: his eyes had grown heavier and he was oblivious to me. By the time I got to visual flight rules, Mr. Varne's eyes had begun to fill with tears and he was crying silently.

Even Father seemed to detect it because he frowned a little, looking around the basement uncertainly.

Gigi ran over and put her arms around him. "There, there, Mr. Varne, you've had a rough time of it. You poor thing."

To our dismay, Mr. Varne put his head in his hands and began to sob. His shoulders shook under the Dallas Cowboys T-shirt.

No one, of course, knew what to do. Being the closest to him, Gigi massaged his shoulders in hopes of soothing him.

A self-conscious silence pervaded the basement.

Finally, Mother spoke.

"Mr. Varne," she said in a voice that to me was overly harsh. "Mr. Varne, you've been through hell, there's no denying that. I'm sure there is a great temptation now to feel overwhelmed. To ask 'Why me?' But you are going to stop crying now. And in the coming days you are not going to feel sorry for yourself. You are going to sit and sit and sit and think of nothing and no one. Then it will come to you that your life is as it is," she said in a matter-of-fact tone as though she were giving out a recipe for baking bread. "And when you know that like you know your own hand, you will no longer have to worry. You will be among the fortunate."

I couldn't believe that this preposterous statement had come from my mother.

Gigi gave a little shriek. "What a coldhearted thing to say," she wailed and began to cry herself. While Gigi put her hands over her eyes, Mr. Varne raised his tearstained face. Was it my imagination or was there a flicker of understanding, a hint that something in the gibberish Mother had just uttered struck him as a rope to grab on to?

Father didn't seem to be aware of Mr. Varne's reaction. Mother's goofy pronouncement had been the last straw for him. His face contracted in anger. "For God's sake, Ayela." He frowned at Mother, and then he turned a contrite heart to our guest. "You'll have to forgive us, Mr. Varne," he said with a mixture of admiration and helplessness, unable to explain what for or why. He shook his head and put his beer down on the washing machine. "You'll just have to forgive us."

It was left to me to take matters in hand. How ironic that I would emerge as the champion of our unfortunate guest. Thinking that a quick exit would be the perfect solution, I stood up and in my gentlest voice asked Mr. Varne if he would like me to drive him back now.

"Alright," he said.

Mother handed him a box with clothes he might need immediately. "We'll set the rest of these things aside for you. Next time you come back, we'll tackle the storeroom," she said as though Mr. Varne knew that was the inner sanctum of Linde detritus.

"Wait just a minute," said Father. He disappeared upstairs and returned with an envelope that he pressed into Mr. Varne's hand. "A little something for you, sir," he said apologetically.

I was apprehensive that once I was alone with Mr. Varne in the car, he would speak freely with me, berating the ridiculous and condescending ways of the Linde family. But Mr. Varne barely said a word. He looked out the window with his chin resting on his hand. The vibes coming from him were not hostile, nor were they despondent, and we rode along in a tentative silence.

From time to time I stole a look at him. How could he not be feeling resentful of the scene he had fled? The least I could do was commiserate with him. "My folks are meddlers, always trying to impose their own ways on people," I said, laughing nervously. I couldn't gauge Mr. Varne's reaction, but assuming he couldn't be anything else but in agreement, I went on. "My brothers and I couldn't get out of the house fast enough," I confided to Mr. Varne. "They mean well, I suppose, but Father's so ingratiating it's embarrassing," I added. "And she's so blasted weird." I thought I saw an inspiring nod of agreement from Mr. Varne. Like a fool, I plunged headlong into a litany of my parents' sins: how my mother had basically ruined my brother Xavier's life; how my father had abandoned us for one year to go work on some dingbat railroad in Bolivia or somewhere; the way neither ever accepted my flying or my wives, and on and on.

As there was no response from Mr. Varne, I eventually shut up. I began to think that perhaps I had gone too far. Riding along, I sensed a gulf had opened up between us, growing ever wider, with Mr. Varne turning calmer, fainter, his presence becoming lighter, moving quietly away from me and the afternoon we had shared.

When we neared Olaca, he spoke up to give me directions to the shelter. But he never said anything of a personal nature. Before he got out of the car, he turned to me, chuckling softly. "Give your folks a break," he said. "And thank your mother for me. Tell her that sandwich iron is fine. Real fine."

13
The Church at Del Rio
1990

From my office window I can see her walking up Dolorosa Street, down Obispo, over toward the square. Back and forth, back and forth, in that old trench coat, her hair down, hands in the pockets.

She took Frederick's death pretty hard. Broke into a rage at the hospital at the way he was being handled during a gag reflex test. I see it all the time. The patient's systems start to break down, the family is confused, helpless, strikes out. Someone is accused of not doing his job properly.

I was Frederick and Ayela's physician for forty years. They were always healthy, but she was tougher, better blood pressure, cholesterol, an extremely low sedimentation rate which meant little or no internal inflammation, and that, they say, is the key. A matter of genes, maybe, but she spouted off, blew out what was bothering her. He was always a little more withheld, more diplomatic. Had that borderline blood pressure, you always worry about stroke and that would have killed him, and her too, to see him vegetate like that.

What happened was bad enough, with his fall there in the woods, tripping over an old tree root, could have happened to anyone, and then the subdural hematoma. It was a textbook case, after the fall he got right up, brushed himself off, continued walking. Everything was fine. Then two weeks later he started slurring his words, and she brought him in. "He hasn't been drinking, Edward, if that's what you think," she said. I brought up the usual suspects, numbness, dizziness, and severe headaches — all negative. My query about whether he'd had any slips or falls gave her pause. Those big eyes of hers widened, registering trepidation. "A fall, yes, a slight thing," she admitted, "but that was weeks ago. Well, perhaps he did hit his head, nothing serious though." She tried to wave it away. She was aghast at the idea of him being admitted to the hospital, balked at the surgery. But at that age, you have to operate and the subdurals can go down pretty quickly. I tried to prepare her. The operation itself was a success. But he had that long recuperation in the hospital, the sepsis set in, and, well, he never recovered. A classic situation.

Of course we knew the Lindes socially too, which always makes the whole business more difficult. In the early days we belonged to the same set. All that changed over time. The Lindes got involved in the Arts Pavilion and the music. Sarah and I weren't so much inclined to those highbrow goings-on, we preferred our golf and our bridge and we drifted toward the country club life. The others went their own ways too. But the early loyalties don't fade. We had fine times back then, those Friday nights when the lot of us got together and virtually drank our dinners, and the dancing. I do remember that the women were all a little afraid of Ayela, you never knew what she was going to do next. The women made nice with her, but deep down they didn't fully trust her. There was always that fear that maybe one of the husbands might confuse unpredictable with exotic and, well, stray. All that seems foolish now, a small concern. She was wonderful, but they all were, back then, all of them, with that luminous skin of youth. She'd been stoic at the funeral, she had the boys with her though, and the grandchildren, and with that brood there were more than enough distractions from death.

Seeing her rattle around town disturbed me, and at dinner one night, I mentioned Ayela's walking habits to my wife, Sarah. "Why doesn't she go to Boston and stay with the boys a while?" I wondered out loud.

"She won't go up there," Sarah said with authority. "She says it's the weather. But I don't know. I just don't think she wants to bother with them now."

"Well, call her up for lunch," I suggested.

"I did. She said she doesn't eat lunch anymore."

"Stubborn. As stubborn as her mother, who spent her last years sitting in the park seething at the world. Ayela has that in her, you can see it in the set of the chin," I told Sarah.

Sarah laughed. "Ayela would hate to be compared to Felidia." She added, "Those two were always at each other's throats. She'll perk up, you'll see. It's only been two months."

Well, fine. I let it pass, and we went on to other things.

But I did keep on eye on Ayela. If I was speaking to a patient in my office, my eye would drift to the window. There she'd be, walking up one side of the street and down the other, around the corner, out of sight, and then inevitably, right back again.

Finally, I called her on the phone and asked her about her health. "It's been better," she said, and I suggested that she come see me in the office and I would prescribe something for her to make it a little easier.

Her voice was firm. "Only if it comes from the woods." She had that history, the grandmother, the witch doctor thing, and the herbs, there's something to it, of course, and with the state of big pharma these days, well, Lord knows, no wonder everyone thinks it's a case of name your poison, the disease or the drug.

Of course, she didn't come round to see me. One day I ran into Concha on the square. Now that Frederick was gone, Concha probably knew Ayela best. She had been her housekeeper forever, and those two were thick as thieves, a good thing too. "She's bad, Dr. Teller," Concha told me. "Just sits in Mr. Frederick's library all day with the door shut. Won't take meals, picks at a little boiled chicken for dinner. When she's not in there, she walks the streets."

"She's had a tough few months. Let's just let her be. The tincture of time and all that," I said in my most confident manner, all the while thinking that Ayela Linde was a house that fire had damaged and if a single board were moved, the whole works might cave in.

"Tell her if she needs me, she knows where to find me," were my parting words to Concha.

Though I didn't really expect it, Ayela Linde did come to my office three weeks later. She refused to been seen in the examining room, and I found her waiting for me in my office. There were dark circles under her eyes, and overall she looked a little haggard. She was not given to small talk, and after we shook hands I put some questions to her about her sleeping patterns, appetite, exercise, depression, all of which she shrugged off, and I wondered why it was that she had come and what she wanted from me.

She seemed ill at ease, shifting her position in the chair, unable to look me in the eye. Abruptly she stood up and began pacing. Funny thing was, she stopped in front of a painting on the far wall, as if that was what she had been looking for all along. After studying it, she brightened. "That's the church at Del Rio," she said, seeming thrilled as a child. As soon as she said that, I remembered that day we had driven down across the border. It must have been forty-five, fifty years ago. Ayela had been wearing a light pink dress that had a sheen to it; I remember it vividly because I had the silly notion that I wanted to run my hand along the dress to see if the sheen might rub off on my fingers. Eight of us had gone in two separate cars. Sarah and I had ridden with the Lindes. Frederick put the top down on the red convertible and he drove fast, singing the Cole Porter numbers of the day, amusing us all. Frederick was very musical, with a talent for it and an appreciation too, always having this singer and that harpist for a small concert at their place, in the garden. He played the piano as well. Ayela was musical, but not in the same way. She liked the livelier rhythms and would be the first to dance, particularly a tango or a samba or one of the Latin dances the rest of us were too stiff-hipped for. For a moment I was held hostage by the memory of the red car roaring along the narrow sun-beaten roads carrying the handsome, noisy, carefree foursome oblivious to all else but our youth.

"Do you remember, Edward, do you remember how we all went down to Del Rio that day?" Ayela went on excitedly. "Xavier was just a baby, we left him with Concha for the day, it was the first time we had been away from him. We drove down, the pack of us, you and Sarah had just married, and we had lunch in the café with the yellow-necked parrot that kept saying, 'Get out of here,' in Spanish." She stopped to catch her breath and said, "It was the first time Sarah had tequila." Ayela laughed at the thought, adding, "Sarah is the only woman I know who looks more beautiful after drinking tequila. It releases her from something, I don't know what." Ayela's eyes remained fixed on the painting, with her back to me. "She was beautiful, wasn't she, Edward?"

"Yes, she was," I agreed. I didn't know where Ayela was going with all this, I doubt if she did herself, but the morose feeling in the office lifted with the shift in her mood, so I played along. We spoke of the others too, Lee Hollister and his wife Betty Fay, Horty Drenk and her husband, and buying the beaded necklaces the Indians sold on the side of the street, the intoxicating smell of the rosemary bushes at the mercado, the small details that cross the border of memory. Ayela reminded me that Lee Hollister had wandered away from us and given the beggar children standing around the church doorway ten American dollars, a grand sum in those days. In turn, I brought up something that she had forgotten: how she had spotted the painting of the church at Del

Rio in the midst of a few other canvases piled up against an overflowing trash can at the little gas station where we stopped on the way home.

"You saw it, raved about it, and then decided not to take it. So I picked it up. Do you remember?" I asked her.

"Oh, did I? Really?" she said absently, her eyes still on the painting.

I had always liked that painting, it was probably not done by a professional artist, but certainly by someone with the ability to feel the essence of things. The painting was simple, just as the church was, a goldish stone with a single blunted spire standing humbly beneath the cloudless sky in the heat of the Mexican sun. Though I'm not a religious man, the painting had always seemed to me the perfect expression of, well, sanctity, for lack of a better word.

Ayela stepped toward the painting, seeming to want to examine it more closely.

I waited for her to speak.

"Do you know something about that day we went down to Del Rio, Edward?" she asked me.

"No, what?"

"In the morning before we started out, I told Frederick I was leaving him because he could not make me happy. Can you imagine? Can you imagine saying such a dreadful thing to a man like that?"

I must confess that I was as surprised as she was distraught. As marriages go, we all thought theirs was one of the better ones, that they had kept the passion alive far longer than they had a right to.

"We all say things we don't mean," I tried to console her.

"I was always threatening that," she said quietly.

It was the kind of admission that made me want to race back to the world of blood counts and creatinine levels and albumin and uric acid. An ordered world, where I felt at home and in control of putting a name on what had gone wrong. Yet cursed with the inclination to fix what seemed to be broken, I suffered on. I tried a dismissive laugh. "Oh, you should hear what Sarah says to me."

"We are different, Sarah and I. Very different," Ayela said, her voice full of insinuation that I dared not breach. She still had her back to me, so I did not even have the advantage of seeing the face, which was often a better measure of illness than a patient's words. The wrinkling of a brow, the fear in the eyes, the tone of the skin, these were the indicators that revealed the inner condition.

"Yes," was all I managed to say. "Yes, you are different, you and Sarah." I said it in as neutral a voice as I could muster, feeling that I was heading into uncertain and probably dangerous territory.

"I would have given anything to be more like Sarah," she blurted out.

Women have always mystified me, the workings of their minds, the circuitous route their thoughts take to get from point A to point B. Theirs is nonlinear logic, and I shuddered at the various ways this admission of Ayela's might have been interpreted. Yet if I learned anything from half a century of doctoring, it was to anticipate three steps ahead of what was being said. It's not so difficult, really. There are only so many things that we humans desire, and by the time we're out of childhood, we all know what they are. Whether we're willing to admit it is another matter.

Actually, I thought I saw what she was getting at with all this, and made a bold statement: "Frederick loved you very much, Ayela. Everyone knew that." I told her that because she needed to hear it, but also because I knew it to be true.

My gamble paid off. Her shoulders began to shake violently. I had never seen Ayela Linde cry. It was a silent cry, which was unexpected, not at all like the opposite of her laugh, which was a boisterous, gutsy thing. She put her hand over her eyes, as one might do to shade them from the sun. I didn't hear a sound, though I knew she was crying from the shaking of her shoulders. Finally, she turned to me, saying through her tears, "I never thought it would be this hard."

"We never do," I said and let her cry in peace. I continued to sit in my doctor's chair, assuming what I hoped was a benevolent air. There was nothing further to be done. Tears were the sign that the patient had exercised the greater knowledge of her own needs. Still, I wrote her a prescription, and pressed in into her hand as we said good-bye.

I told her to try and be more social, get out more, see people, take up a hobby.

"Come round for dinner some night, won't you?"

"Yes," she said, though we both knew she wouldn't.

"Well, at least give me a call and let me know how you're doing," I said to her. Patients never think it makes a difference to us, but it does. Ego is involved of course, if you were on the mark in your diagnosis and treatment. But there's many a night their maladies come back to me. This one's rheumatism, does it still ache? That one with the strange bowel infection, is it still giving him trouble? That they don't come back doesn't mean they're cured and, well, we wonder.

To my surprise, about a month later Sarah and I received an invitation for dinner at the home of Ayela Linde. The invitation was written with black ink on plain parchment paper and gave no hint as to the occasion. Sarah thought it might be some kind of memorial for Frederick, so we both dressed in dark, serious clothes.

Concha answered the door and led us out to the patio, where Ayela was entertaining two others. It took me a while to recognize who they were, and when I had added it up, I was struck by Ayela's gesture to gather the old gang, or what was left of it, those who had made the trip to Del Rio that we had spoken of in my office. It seemed an exceptionally sweet and tender thing to do.

Ayela jumped up to welcome us. She was wearing some long yellowish thing and there was a radiance about her that seemed more than superficial. Ayela embraced Sarah and me in turn, as Horty Drenk and Bill Hollister shouted their hellos, and there was much kissing and clapping of shoulders among us.

"When was the last time we all got together?" Horty Drenk exclaimed.

"Well, it must be thirty, thirty-five years now. Too long," Sarah replied.

Even though we remained in the Santa Rosalia area, our set had disbanded a few years after that Del Rio outing, going the way life called us. The Drenks went religious on us, and the Hollisters, well, they had all they could do to do to stay afloat financially. Now we were in our seventies, some of us pushing eighty. Physically, Horty Drenk had taken the worst beating. I was surprised to see she used a walker, and that she had taken up residence at the Infirmary of the Good Shepherd after her husband had passed away five years ago. She looked old and worn out. Her upper arms were very wrinkled. Her brown hair was frowsy, arranged in no discernible style, and the light dress she was wearing might have been made of an old bedsheet. The slight sour smell of aging was all over her.

I looked from Horty to Sarah. Sarah's blondish hair had a little help from the hairdresser every week, but she liked doing that, to keep herself up, paint her nails, make up, spend the money on all that female frippery. I was always grousing about the bills, berating her for the unnecessary expense. I'm semi-retired, and we don't have endless resources, I'd tell her, but after seeing Horty's decline, I silently blessed my wife for ignoring my objections and doing what she wanted. I moved my chair closer to Sarah's to be in the comforting aura of her perfume, and a feeling of remorse for all my complaining welled up in me. On an impulse I reached for Sarah's hand and raised it to my lips.

That delighted Horty. "How sweet! He was always wild about you," Horty crowed.

"Always," I agreed, feeling a little ashamed of myself for the sentiments that had inspired my gallantry.

Horty set about rummaging through her purse. Unearthing a dog-eared envelope, she removed two Mass cards for her husband, Phil, and passed one each to Sarah and me. "I wanted you to have these, as you couldn't make it to the funeral," she said with just a trace of bitterness.

I murmured my thanks, though surprised that she was still doing this after such a long time.

"You're looking well for someone your age, Doc," Bill Hollister told me. He was always the joker type, big, ruddy, and cursed with a little too much taste for the booze. He had had several jobs, never quite seeming to find his groove as they say, then I heard he had made good rather late in life on a land deal on the other side of the border. I hadn't known he had lost his Betty Fay to colon cancer.

"I see you're able to sit up and take nourishment," I countered. Bill's eyes had the bloodshot look of high blood pressure, but he appeared trim and vigorous enough. His light blue golf shirt and light blue plaid cotton slacks and white shoes pegged him as a man who logs in many miles at the mall. "Ayela here tracked me down up in Laredo." He smiled proudly. "I moved up there to be closer to my youngest, Evvy Jane."

Ayela brought out the photo albums, and we reminisced about old times.

The trip down to Del Rio came up, of course, but it was eclipsed by the flood of other good times we had had together. The Hollisters' Christmas party, the concert Frederick had given for the harpist from Grenada, the time we all dressed up in white for some celebration or other. Frederick and Phil Drenk in a rowboat somewhere.

"That was up at Bilou Lake," Bill Hollister said. "Just before they capsized!"

"What sailors they were!" Ayela let loose with her big laugh.

Horty Drenk nearly spit out her fruit punch at that. "This is fun," she said.

It was fun. We all felt it. The five of us took to horsing around like we did in the old days, chiding each other, accepting our shortcomings as inevitable and unimportant as a rain shower. To be with people whom you had known and who had known you nearly half a century had an unnervingly moving effect.

Feeling expansive, I called for Concha. "Bring us all another round of those delicious drinks, will you, dear? And sit down yourself and join us," I said perhaps too loudly.

Ayela seconded the motion. "Yes, do, Concha. You can tell us all what fools we were back then," she said good-naturedly.

"Señora, don't get me started," Concha replied, in her wry way declining the invitation, and setting down a platter of small tortillas and other finger foods.

Horty Drenk took two tortillas. "Phil never liked these. I can't imagine why not," she said between mouthfuls.

"Save some for the rest of us, Horty," Bill Hollister teased.

"God helps those who help themselves," Horty shot back.

"Stop it you two, we've got work to do here," Ayela said, and put yet another album on the table.

Ayela's photo albums were arranged chronologically, and we pored over every picture, like children trying to outdo each other at what we could remember. We went through three albums like this, eating, drinking, and sparring until we were besotted with our past. On the last pages of the last album were photos of the men going out to hunt white-winged doves, and the women in a line, doing the cancan, and one silly one of the lot of us in sombreros so big you could hardly make out the faces.

We were squabbling over who might be who, when Horty Drenk abruptly set down her glass. "I wish the others were with us," she said fiercely.

No one dared say a word or look at Ayela, as her loss was the freshest.

I cast about for some soothing words to throw out, silently praying that Sarah would bail us out. She was better at these things, and usually took it upon herself to intervene when situations got sticky.

"We're all going home eventually," she said finally in her gentle voice. "Some of us just left the party earlier."

"I'm ready," Bill Hollister exclaimed.

Horty Drenk swatted him on the arm. "Never give up, you old goat!" she said, and everyone laughed, relieved to be rid of the thought of death.

From that point, though, the party took on a quieter air. Ayela and I spoke about how the old section of town had gone seedy. Sarah and Bill Hollister and Horty talked about what all the children of our old set had gotten up to.

Around ten, we all seemed to have run out of gas.

Bill Hollister looked at his watch. "We would have just been gearing up about now," he said.

"Well, now we're old," Ayela said. "We're a bunch of old fogies with aches and pains and no desire to stay up past nine o'clock."

She intended flippancy, I'm sure of it, because that was her way, and because she seemed to be enjoying herself immensely. Even though we all knew what we were and where we were headed, the words were harsh and they hung in the air, flooring us with their accuracy.

Bill Hollister examined his fingernails and Horty Drenk began to fuss with her purse. In Sarah I recognized that catwalk between calm and tears. Even Ayela had nothing further to say.

Sitting there in the warm night air on the Lindes' patio strung with colored lanterns, the certainty that the five of us would never again be together suddenly became overwhelming. We might see one another on the street or in a store, but another night like tonight, never. In this evening we had been given a special reprieve, we all knew that and no one proposed that it be repeated.

Finally, Sarah broke the silence. "You're not headed back to Laredo tonight, are you, Bill?"

"No, no. I've taken a room at the Hotel del Norte," he said distractedly.

Ayela inquired whether Horty needed a ride back to the home.

"We'll be glad to take her," I volunteered.

"Well then," Horty Drenk said, and started to rise from the table. It took her a few minutes to collect her purse and get the walker in position. The rest of us stood up as well and tried not to walk too fast as Horty shuffled out toward the front door.

Ayela insisted on accompanying us to our cars.

As Horty was about to brave the task of wedging herself into our backseat, she took both Ayela's hands in hers. "Thanks, deary, you've given us a gift. You're always doing these things, you're so . . . so . . . ." Horty broke off in an effort to hold back the tears.

"Thank Edward," said Ayela, nodding in my direction. "He's the sentimentalist. He's got that silly old painting of the church at Del Rio on his office wall." Ayela laughed that unruly laugh of hers, which left us all on an up note. We said our good-byes, and she turned back toward the house. I stood by the car, watching her make her way up the front walk. I thought she might turn around and give us one last wave, but she didn't. By the time she reached the door, I can't be sure, but I thought I saw her shoulders shaking, just slightly.

14
That Old Lady
1995

She started coming in June, sitting there on the bench by a big banyan tree, staring into space, watching the song sparrows hop around the ground, staring off, watching the sparrows. All afternoon, just sitting there. She stood out to me because of the way she dressed. Squint and she looked like a hippie girl, long flowery skirts and some kind of shirt with beads. But she was old. Her hair was almost white and there were wrinkles on her cheeks, even on her arms. An old lady. Somebody's grandmother.

When six o'clock comes, I want to leave immediately. I've got my routine. Lock up the big iron gates of the Botanical Garden, hang up the tan jumpsuit uniform, the old iron keys, put the strongbox under the wood desk, punch out, pull the gatehouse door shut.

It was a Thursday in July, right after the Fourth. I came back from locking up the front gate and there she was, still sitting on her bench next to the path, as though she didn't have any idea of the time. She could've gotten me in real trouble, being locked in here all night.

I went over to her. "Ma'am, don't you know what time it is?"

She didn't even look at me. "I'm a widow," she said. "I have no use for time." It was a sad thing to say, but she didn't seem sad. She didn't have a big mush face that was weak around the mouth. She wasn't a crier, like some of the old ladies that come here.

Something made me feel sorry for her, just the same, sitting alone like that with nowhere to go. "Don't you have to get home now?" I asked her. She looked up and stared at me. "My husband has been dead for five years," she said.

"Sorry."

She didn't answer me.

"That's too bad," I said. The silence was driving me bonkers.

She just sat there, staring away.

"I mean, it's too bad, if you loved him and all."

Nothing from her.

I waved my hand in front of her face. She looked up at me but didn't speak. So I did. "Okay, well, then, I'll tell you my story. My momma didn't love my pa. She threw him out. Called him shiftless. 'Get out of here twice,' she told him, 'and don't come back.' My momma wouldn't have cared if he fell down a hole. She'd have been happy, danced a jig. So it ain't always a bad thing when the old man is gone."

Not even a blink from her.

"Well," I started in again, trying to explain myself. "I

just mean it could be kind of a bummer for you if you dug the guy."

She didn't take the bait. She just batted away the bugs that were buzzing around her head.

"So did you?"

"Did I what?"

"Love the guy?"

She sighed. "Everybody loved Frederick."

"You included?"

She sighed again. "Oh, that man could be exasperating. He always had to have things just so. The salt crackers that I had to drive over to that little market in Oderada for, 'They're behind the bread, near the canned peas,' he'd say, twenty miles for those damn crackers and I'd chase all over that market up and down the aisles just looking for them, nearly mad with annoyance, they weren't there, I was convinced, cursing him for making me drive all that way for such a little thing when I had the children, when I had so many other things to do, to get, to be." She stopped to catch her breath. "And then I'd come upon the crackers, just like he said, behind the bread, in front of the canned peas. And I'd stop, a little ashamed of myself and I'd think, why yes, why shouldn't he have those salt crackers with his martinis in the evenings, why shouldn't he have whatever he wants. He's a good man." She looked away.

Then she started up again. "And do you know what they did? Do you know what they had the nerve to do in the hospital?"

"I guess you're going to tell me."

"I hadn't turned my back for a minute. I just went down to the cafeteria to get some of that vile coffee. When I came back he was gone. They had taken him somewhere for another test. Finally, I found him, he was in some dingy room in his wheelchair. His back was to me. But when you've lived with a man for nearly fifty years you know the back of his head!" Then I thought she was gonna cry for sure. "That fine silvered head, with the hair all tufted and matted from lying against the pillow," she said, looking sad. "I turned his wheelchair around, and there he was with blue liquid drooling out of his mouth and dribbling down his chin and onto his hospital gown. You should have seen his eyes. Those strong blue eyes, so, so helpless. But of course he couldn't speak a word. And those silly nurses, standing on the other side of the room like they were on a coffee break. Cackling about a television show. They stopped short when they saw me, alright. Stopped short and snapped to attention. 'The patient is having a test, the doctor will give you the results later,' the one with the earrings said. Can you imagine?"

"Well, that was a long time ago," she said, winding down like a balloon losing air. "I don't know what got me started on all that."

Then both of us were just staring into space.

"Yeah, hospitals suck," I said finally.

She looked up at me surprised, like I had said the smartest thing in the world. "Yes," she said. "Yes, they do." She kept on smiling at me like I was a genius or something.

"Well, ma'am, I've got to get going."

"Shh," she said. "Listen."

"Listen to what . . . the sound of nothing going on?"

"Be still. Can't you feel the droning?"

I tried. "Well, sort of." I had to say that it felt like something, something low and spooky that was always there.

"It's ruination," she said. "See the fruit in the trees, getting heavy, heavier. Sagging with the weight of their ripeness. You can just feel it. Pretty soon they'll fall to the ground, and the animals will come along and eat the rotting fruit and leave the stones scattered on the ground like little lost brains."

"Man, that's gross."

"Be still. Just look at those flowers. The scarlet one over there, and the yellow. Past their prime. Indecent, like overage harlots."

She was scaring me now. "You're not some weirdo, are you?"

She just laughed. "Probably." Her teeth were pretty, big too, not horse teeth, but teeth that were made for smiling. She must have been nice-looking once.

Okay, good for her. Be a weirdo all you want, lady, but it's time for me to get high, zip around on my motorcycle, hit on some chicks, shoot some pool down at Blo's. Maybe get in a fight. Yeah, a fight. "Hey, come on, ma'am, it's nearly seven now. I've got to go, which means you've got to go too."

She didn't budge. "What's your hurry? Your wife and children are expecting you?"

"Lady, I'm only nineteen. I don't have anything like a wife."

"I see," she said. "Well, perhaps you're meeting your colleagues for a drink."

"Huh? I just want to get out of here." This place gives me the creeps, especially after closing time.

"Don't be silly. It's lovely here. It's a wonderful place to work."

"Yeah, you and my parole officer ought to get together and gush over it."

"Parole officer?" She looked sideways at me. "Are you a murderer?"

"Stole a car."

"Well, you shouldn't be doing that kind of thing, young man."

"It was a red Corvette, the new C5 Corvette, the greatest Corvette ever, and a convertible. Just sitting there on the street, day after day, no one using it. That's the crime," I told her. I didn't expect an answer but she sat there chewing over what I said.

"Well, yes," she said slowly. "I see what you mean."

"Really?" I couldn't believe my ears.

"In a manner of speaking, yes."

Finally, someone who saw it my way. In gratitude I offered her a cigarette.

"No, thank you, I don't smoke. And neither should you, young man." All of a sudden she reached under the bench and started rummaging through the shopping bags she had stashed there. She took out a small cloth and laid it on the bench, put some cheese and crackers on a china plate and took out a thermos. "I'm sorry, I hadn't expected you. Would you mind drinking from a paper cup?" She didn't even wait for an answer, she just fumbled around her bags for a large red paper cup and a green bottle and started pouring.

"Wine? Al-right!" I said, for a minute forgetting where I was.

"Yes, I'm glad you could join me for cocktails."

"Whoa, whoa, whoa, lady. What do you think you're doing?!" I started walking back and forth. "It's after closing time and it's going to get dark soon. They'll fire me if they find me."

She looked at me like I was a pitiful child having a tantrum over a lollipop. "Oh, don't worry about that," she said. "I would never let that happen."

"Just how are you going to do that?!" I was getting real worked up now.

"I have some pretty good connections," she said in a weird kind of soothing voice. "Now, tell me about that tattoo on your forearm. It's a crow, is it not? I'm always curious to know why young people want to do that to their gorgeous skin."

Now she was digging for something else in those bags of hers. "As I said, I wasn't expecting you. But I'll be happy to share whatever I have. Do you like cold chicken?"

"Ma'am, ma'am! You're getting crazy here. This is a public botanical garden. And it's closed. And I'm responsible for closing it. Getting everybody out."

"Yes. I know you are. And you've done an excellent job."

"But you're still here!"

"Yes." She smiled. "Isn't it grand?"

"No. No, it is not grand. If someone sees us coming out of here at night I'm busted."

She shot me a dirty look. "Do you think I would jeopardize your job?" She started putting some cheese slabs on the crackers. "Now listen," she said to me, lowering her voice like someone might overhear us. "No one will see us coming out at night because I'll be walking out the front gate in broad daylight, just as a regular guest would. Tomorrow."

"What?! You're going to stay here all night? Sleep here?"

She started for those bags again and this time she pulled out a pillow and blanket. "I've always loved sleeping outdoors," she said. "It makes one closer to heaven."

"Ma'am, ma'am. You can't do that. I'm calling the cops right now."

"But young man, I thought we saw eye to eye. You steal a convertible because it was just sitting there, and that's the crime. Well, here is a lovely, no, a spectacular garden that no one is in, and it's just sitting here. That's the crime, is it not?"

"Oh my God, lady! Now I know you're nuts." I turned to walk toward the gate, but the faster I walked the less I wanted to squeal on her. I should have just kept going, let myself out and never thought of her again. But it's not every day you meet a crazy old coot like her. And I didn't really have anywhere to go.

She barely noticed I was standing right in front of her again. She was too busy sipping her cocktail and humming a tune and fingering some pink flower petals she picked up off the ground.

I cleared my throat.

She looked up. "Oh, it's you. Having second thoughts about turning me in?"

"Sort of," I admitted.

She started fussing with the food again. "You must be hungry."

"Oh, alright," I said. "Just for a minute or two, and then you're on your own," I warned her and sat down on the ground.

"Ah, that's better. It's nice to have a little change of scene every now and then, don't you think?"

I didn't answer and we sat in silence munching on the chicken. It was getting on to eight o'clock. The air was cooler. All those gigantic trees were getting dark, gray, black. The flowers were shutting up, bugs flying this way and that. There was a lot of stirring and rearranging going on like the whole place was getting ready to bear down on us and squash us flat. Not that I could see anything, I could just feel it, they way you know something's going on behind your back. It gave me a little chill, but of course I wasn't going to tell her.

"Do you like chocolate seven-layer cake?" she asked, putting a piece on my plate. "Ah, this is the best part of the day," she said. "When it starts to get dark, the bugs will sting the birds. Bats will come out and swallow the bugs. Flower petals will drop off one by one. The owl will begin its descent. Under the shadows, the whole place will be in glorious decay."

She went on and on about the decay and rot like I wasn't even here. Making all the gross details sound so great, so important. It was bumming me out. Shut up, I wanted to scream, shut up! But I have manners, so I started humming, trying to drown her out. When I couldn't hold it in any longer I just let the tears fall, filling up the little craters in the cake with salty puddles. She didn't even notice I was crying. Okay, maybe I wanted her to, so I made a little crying squeak, like a stepped-on mouse.

She broke right off what she was saying. "What's the matter?"

"I hate rot," I managed to push out. By then I was really losing it, shoulders heaving up and down, sobbing.

"Tell me," she said softly.

"You want to hear a good rot story?" I blathered away, not looking at her. "I'll tell you about my ma. She's rotting away inside. Rotting. She can't work no more. Lies there on the couch all day. Looks like she's got a bad hangover and two black eyes." I started to turn and walk away, then I came back real close to the old lady. "My ma's got no one but me to take care of her. That's why I can't lose this job, lady, don't you see? How am I gonna take care of her? How the hell am I going to do that? I'm not even twenty yet."

Then I just stood there sobbing my head off like a fool.

I could feel her looking at me.

"I'm so sorry," she said in a gentle way.

That made it worse. I couldn't stop bawling to save my skin.

"But you know what?" she said. "It never stops. Not for any of us," she said.

I knew she was still looking at me. I felt that as long as she was watching me I couldn't fall too far down the hole. She waited for me to calm down.

The sun was well gone now and the remaining light was

that no-man's-land color, like a glass of water. It was quiet, but only on the surface.

She patted the bench beside her. "Come, sit by me a minute."

"Oh, alright," I said, still blubbering a bit. "But only if you'll stop talking."

15
The Marvelous Yellow Cage
1999

The shopkeeper who sold it to her said this about the cage: that it came from an old hotel in Veracruz where it hung in the lobby and held jungle birds that were so charmed by the genial voices of the guests and the clink of bar glasses that they sang all day and into the night. When the hotel was razed to make way for a new one, the birds refused to budge from the cage, they pecked to bleeding the hands of anyone who tried to remove them, and sang their last song as the cage was heaved onto the ash pile of the past.

She'd thought it such a fine story. And a splendid cage, domed, yellow, with Victorian curlicues about the sides and base, and large. Large enough to contain a human. In the shop she marveled at the cage, imagining it full of troupials of her own, knowing she had to have it. She bought it at full price without bothering to dicker, but when it was delivered to the house it was all wrong, monstrous even, and she had it put in the storeroom under the acacia tree where it lay forgotten for decades.

That much Ayela Linde remembered right away, it came rushing at her as she opened the door one August afternoon and the yellow form nearly glowed in the dim of the storeroom. Now in her eighties, Ayela Linde was so comfortable with herself and the liberty with which she led her widow's life, free to indulge her midmorning melancholy, her revulsion for television, her preference for the Roman practice of drawing the drapes against the heat of the day, and all the other tics of body and spirit, that not much upset her. The sight of the cage, the size of it, the look of it, however, sent a shudder through her, and her usually fine memory drew a blank as to why she had ever had the urge to purchase such an unreasonable object.

Xavier Linde poked his head in the storeroom door. "Mother, are you in there?"

"Over here," she called, waving. "I'm looking for that alabaster statue for you."

He picked his way through the sea of old armchairs and garden statuary, still in the suit he had worn for twelve hours on the two planes and one ramshackle hired car he had taken to drop in unexpectedly on his mother. Xavier Linde frowned. "Look at all this," he groaned. "Mother, you've got to start weeding it out."

Ayela Linde turned toward her firstborn. He had taken nothing of her, not her caramel skin, her liquid eyes, her instinctive aloofness. He was all his father, the tall frame, the auburn hair, the fastidious appearance, a nature similarly inclined toward the dutiful, but devoid of the father's passionate imagination that long ago captured the fancy and then the heart of Ayela Linde.

With a widow's need to invoke the departed, Ayela Linde summoned her husband: he came to her in his immaculate linen suit striding across the plaza with blueprints for a new wing on the Infirmary of the Good Shepherd, and then sitting under the stars, eyes closed as the tremor of violins rose on the evening air in the amphitheater he had badgered the politicians of Santa Rosalia to build.

At the age of twenty-five, Frederick had known himself, and, breaking free of the stranglehold of three generations of Linde influence, left the Great Depression and the sunless city of Boston with only his law degree and an open heart. He set out overland to South America but stopped when love apprehended him in the form of Santa Rosalia, in which he saw a backwater Spanish colonial town possessed of a certain golden light that flattered its superstitious populace, and lay close enough to the Mexican border to claim the exotic persuasion of a foreign land.

Then, of course, there was herself. She had to smile. What a hard thing she was in those days, willful, haughty, strutting down Dolorosa Street in the flowered dresses of her mother's creation, her breasts, her chin thrust forward, a stranger to soft feelings with no use for the sherbet-colored sky of summer evenings. Even her laugh was a sneering, mocking thing, and in her eyes was a flinty look that both abhorred and craved the insolent stares of the men loitering outside the bars. She was only eighteen when Frederick Linde first laid eyes on her. She remembered that evening as if it were yesterday. He must have seen a spirit that, not unlike his own, hung by a thread to the things of this world. What she needs is a life, he must have said to himself, which gave him courage to approach her as she sat in the twilight on a bench in the plaza, waiting to throw herself away on the men who perfumed the night with their cigars and whiskeyed breath.

Ayela Linde recalled with fondness their proper wedding in the Church of San Lorenzo, a year after their hasty elopement to the justice of the peace, he in a morning suit, she in a Mexican wedding dress, and how they had taken the large stucco house on Olivea Road, where the jacaranda trees were fuller and the heat seemed more bearable. After their wedding trip to Corpus Christi, Frederick had set up a law practice in Santa Rosalia and became a fixture about the limestone courthouse in his white linen suit.

What a good planner he had been, she mused. Early in their marriage he filled her with life three times in measured succession, ensuring that for the next quarter century she was not without the constant bickering and the frenetic love and the sudden insurrections that diverted her mind from its own darker tendencies. When their sons moved away, retreating to their father's native Boston, she viewed it as betrayal. Frederick dismissed it with a casual "Whatever we are, they'll be the opposite," but immediately devoted himself to assuming their place. He began to come home for lunch, insisting on elaborate meals and cheerful company, and requiring her presence at the charitable events he headed in Zaragosa County, and they went on this way, eating kingly concoctions, presiding over music festivals, flying over the land in hot-air balloons to usher in all manner of celebrations until Frederick's death nine years ago.

With those visions of her husband came the courage to

stand up to the petty concerns of her son, and she turned to Xavier, saying, "I'm too old to have someone telling me what to do with my things."

At eight o'clock that evening Ayela Linde, in a dress of blue silk that flowed to her ankles, sat at the head of the dining table, with Xavier to her right. Not since the November weekend six years ago when Freddie's family stopped en route to a diving trip on the island of Cozumel had Ayela Linde seen any of her sons. At this point she was not the kind of mother who required her children's presence, preferring to go it alone lest she be robbed of an old age free from the good intentions of her offspring. Surmising that this lay behind Xavier's trip, she postponed the inevitable and leaned a glowing face toward him: "Tell me about the girls."

With more than a little relief, her son spoke about his own family, the bewildering life of his two teenage daughters and his second wife, Hilaire, an accountant like himself, but with a restlessness she appeased by acting in a local theater troupe when a role sufficiently tragic came along. He nearly forgot himself in the balm of his mother's undivided attention and, in a rush of gratitude, stopped short and put his hand over hers.

"It's good to see you, Mother."

Before Xavier Linde could say something he might later regret, Concha appeared. Dressed in a gray uniform that had grown too big for her, she carried a large platter and the impassive expression of a servant ravenous to learn the situation at the table.

Other evenings, Concha and Ayela Linde ate a bowl of cereal together at five-thirty, seven, nine-fifteen, whenever hunger struck. They sat at the plank table in the kitchen, Ayela reading aloud from the evening paper. But from the first gong of the doorbell and the giddiness that came as her little bird body was twirled around and set gently down by Xavier's sturdy arms, Concha threw her entire being at one nearly impossible task: serving his favorite dinner of ropa vieja. She bristled at Ayela's invitation to join them in the dining room, saying, "Let us not ruin Mr. Xavier's memories."

As they ate Ayela Linde spoke of the goings on in Santa Rosalia. Her son listened, keenly aware of the intelligence in his mother's voice, her dignified beauty, the white hair that was long and wild in a charming way, part of it caught at the back in a tortoiseshell barrette, as she had always worn it. He began to have second thoughts about the business that he, as the eldest son, was obliged to undertake.

But as Concha finally cleared the plates and water ran and pots thunked in the kitchen, Xavier Linde sat up straighter in his chair and cleared his throat.

"Mother, we want you to come and live with us in Boston."

Ayela laughed as if a child were making a joke. "But darling, I live here," she said.

"We've talked about this before. It's time now." Softening his words, he hastened to add, "We worry about you down here. If you should need anything . . . we'd be right there to take care of you."

Ayela Linde fingered the ornate handle of her silver fork. "But there's Concha." Xavier Linde examined his mother carefully. He spoke gently as if breaking bad news to the next-of-kin. "Concha is . . . old. She's failing. She's probably older than you are, if anyone really knew." He put his hand over hers. "We have the room. It will be better for everyone."

"Mmmmmmm," Ayela Linde replied. She had no intention of spending her last years in the cold, dreary place that her husband had disavowed long ago, where winter lasted for nine months and brown beans and salted cod were standard fare.

Mistaking his mother's silence for miraculous assent, Xavier dared to go on. "I've made some inquiries . . . and the realtor has a buyer for the house."

"But I've left the house to Concha, it's in my will."

"Concha would rattle around here all by herself," Xavier replied.

"It's her home too." Ayela Linde looked thoughtfully at her son. "And it's what I want."

The candlelight flattered her, melting away the years until Xavier saw her on those remote nights of his boyhood, lingering at the dinner table, listening to her husband speak of business matters, idly running her finger through the candle flame. He had thought her strange and reckless, knowing even then that if he didn't take a stand against her, he would never find himself.

Xavier Linde put down his napkin and rose from the table. "Boston's not a bad place, Mother. You'll get to like it," he said and, brushing his lips over his mother's forehead, went up to bed.

After dinner, Concha brought out the coffee and the pralines and the two women sat on the terrace listening to the soft thud of bugs against the bougainvillea.

Despite the heat, they enjoyed their nightly ritual. The night was kind to them, obscuring their wrinkled faces, making them young again. They were grateful and used it for sitting and dreaming and divulging the hopes of their past, either sighing with regret or dying of laughter until their will to be awake trailed off. Together, they rose to ready the kitchen for morning with fresh napkins and bone-white coffee cups overturned on their saucers like gleaming mountains, and made their way upstairs.

Without intending to they had slipped into the ways of an old married couple with such ease and mutual delight that it sometimes struck Ayela Linde like a thorn in the heart and caused her to reconsider whether what she had known during fifty-four years of marriage to Frederick Linde could actually be called love.

"You are going to Boston, then?" Concha asked when she could no longer stand the silence between them.

Ayela laughed. "That's what the boys seem to think."

"Perhaps that is best."

"What about you?"

"I will be alright."

"There is no one to care for you."

"Señora, there is."

"Who?"

"There is someone. There is always someone." It was a lie and they both knew it, just as they knew what made it a lie had nothing to do with the fact that as a girl Concha fled from her home on the ravaged Napo River, shorn of its trees and its caterwauling monkeys into a frightening silence, eventually landing in the Linde household as a cook and nursemaid, seeing the family through the raising of three sons and the death of the father and all the raucous joys and sorrows in between with such single-minded devotion she had forgotten to have a life of her own.

Ayela Linde smiled at the liar, waiflike in the ill-fitting uniform, her short iron-gray hair tucked behind the ears, her ancient face lit by innocence. "Come with me."

Concha shook her head. "No. There is no room."

"There is room. We can live together, like here," Ayela Linde suggested, knowing full well the irreplaceable sanctity of here. Here, they rarely went off the property. During the day they played cards, worked in the garden, drank cold chamomile tea, nearly collapsed from scouring the terra-cotta tiles or polishing the heavy English furniture, fell asleep in the coolest spot on the terrace, read to each other the latest anti-aging miracles from the health magazines and the Spanish dime novels from half a century ago and, when the sun was down, took solace in their own muddied versions of the past. Occasionally they felt the urge to cook the old complicated dishes Frederick had requested, and gave themselves over to grinding pine nuts and roasting quails and coaxing the bitterness from eggplants and baking rings of meringue to the perfection of clouds kissed by the sun, after which a dozen dazzling platters appeared on the dining room table. Since their shrunken stomachs couldn't digest what they had so laboriously prepared, they hung the colored lights and threw open the doors to the delight of the neighbors.

"No, not Boston," Concha said. "Think of our life here. Mr. Xavier will understand. He is the one with the heart of an angel."

Ayela Linde reached for the pralines as though she hadn't heard a word.

"You told Mr. Xavier what we want," Concha pressed her. "What did he say?"

Without looking up, Ayela rearranged the uneaten candies on her plate. "Mr. Xavier says we're a couple of ridiculous old women."

For the next three days, on the terrace, over café con leche, in the heat of the afternoon, mother and son debated their future plans in sessions that veered from the quiet and thoughtful to near shouting matches. The endless sessions took their toll on Ayela Linde. A fluttering heart, pains in her hip, sudden and disturbing lapses in memory, and other real and imaginary capitulations to old age began to bother her. In the middle of a restless night, she went for a cup of tea and tripped on the stairs in a fall that did no physical harm but so unnerved her that, when Xavier burst from his room and ran to her aid, she let herself be led to an armchair and soothed and scolded and, feeling as defenseless as a newborn, surrendered in a whisper: "Alright. You win."

The next afternoon a black truck with "Antiques and Estates" printed discreetly in red pulled up in the back drive. Ayela Linde was summoned outside and, standing by the gardens she started with a finicky tea rose given to her by her husband for her twenty-second birthday, was introduced by her son to the truck's owner. Mr. Aguilera, a short man with vigorous arms, closed his eyes and bowed, proclaiming it an honor to meet the distinguished lady who had tended to Santa Rosalia as if it were her own child. Having lost the habit of social discourse, and always uneasy with a preposterously inflated compliment, Ayela Linde muttered an embarrassed thank-you, while recognizing the man for what he was: a vulture.

Mr. Aguilera knew the Linde family by reputation as discerning in their taste, and he leered at the handsome Spanish colonial house as if it were a woman to whom he would soon have unlimited access. Then his eyes fell on the proud, downhearted face of Ayela Linde, and the desire to console her overtook him. What came out was the statement, delivered as he examined cuticles edging their ragged way over his fingernails but in a tone that made her take notice: "You have raised wonderful roses, señora."

She nodded and led him inside and up to the attic, returning to sit in the kitchen where Concha was preparing purple coneflowers for a medicinal tea. Without the vaguest notion of what would become of her, Concha waited with the patience of God in her dark Andean eyes, praying to the holy mother to help her lay flowers along the burdensome path of Ayela Linde and, in a fierce whisper, vowed to them both, "As long as the Lord gives me life I will serve you."

An hour later Mr. Aguilera appeared in the kitchen, still writing in the small blue notebook. Ayela led him outside to the storeroom. From the doorway she watched him defile with his intentions the statue of the one-armed Venus de Milo she sketched while pregnant with Xavier so that he would see beauty in imperfection, the nineteenth-century globe she insisted on so the boys would know the world before it became smaller and less mysterious, the oil painting of St. Peter's Basilica she bought impulsively in a curio shop in Laredo when the bells of the Angelus floating over the sun-baked streets made her painfully aware of the hollowness of her own being.

"Where did that cage come from?" he interrupted her thoughts.

"I don't remember," she said offhandedly, realizing that it hadn't made her shudder as it had a few days earlier. Its effect on her was so benign that she walked over and ran her fingers along its thick iron spokes nubby with yellow paint, thinking of the birds singing their hearts out inside its cavernous womb. She didn't hear Mr. Aguilera say it wasn't a fine piece, just a curiosity.

Mr. Aguilera raised his voice, "Señora, I'm ready to make an offer."

Ayela Linde walked out of the storeroom. The impending loss of her possessions made her dizzy, and Mr. Aguilera feared by the sudden wobble to her gait that she was about to have a fainting spell or worse. He asked whether she wanted a glass of water, when a light came into her eyes. "I don't wish to sell," she said.

Mr. Aguilera protested. "But your son. He said to take the things away today."

The reminder of her son's presumptuousness strengthened her resolve. Ayela Linde repeated her refusal to sell.

"As you wish, señora." He bowed and retreated, thinking Xavier Linde was going to have his hands full.

At six-thirty Xavier Linde stood in front of a pay phone on Dolorosa Street. Having just come from the realtors where he arranged for the sale of the house with the power of at-torney he had insisted be drawn up after his father's death, his heart should have been lighter. But he was plagued by the truth that the brothers' plans for their mother came from selfishness and selflessness, wisdom and foolishness, not in equal parts but in proportions that seemed to shift and re-fract by the minute, the hour, the day, as impossible to pin down as sunlight falling on water.

His brothers hadn't helped matters. He had telephoned them his news, which was met by a cheer from Freddie and from Jesse a chorus of "Hallelujah!" that struck a sour note with Xavier. He hung up convinced it was a bungled busi-ness and that the three of them were about to introduce their mother to the worst years of her life.

"Christ," he muttered, knowing he would never make peace with himself on the matter.

He stood on Dolorosa Street, unsure of where to go next.

Behind the line of stores, his eye fell on the familiar dark three-story façade of the Jesuit school from which he had graduated forty-two years ago with high honors and a tem-porary sense of self-sacrifice. The building was a plain brown stone, the only dark structure in all of Santa Rosalia, and the sight of it flooded him with memories, the strongest of which was on a Friday afternoon in the empty cobblestone courtyard in a light spring rain. Feeling a strange radiance in being wet and cold and alone, he vowed to forsake the material world and like his namesake, Saint Francis Xavier, walk barefoot amid the pearl fisheries of India with the word of God on his lips. The ingenuousness of the fantasy still moved him, and he stood staring into the Dolorosa

Street traffic dreaming of himself before the world got hold of him.

Xavier Linde returned to the house with a bottle of tequila in a paper bag and in an irritable state, and found his mother and Concha drinking lemonade on the terrace. They were not ready to take in his presence. Even after he asked what had happened with Mr. Aguilera, his mother had to finish her laughter before she looked at him with a distracted "I told him to wait. I'm having second thoughts."

"Oh, for God's sake. Just sell it! We're lucky to have someone cart this junk away," Xavier Linde shouted with such surprising sharpness that Concha fled into the house.

Xavier ran his fingers through his thinning hair, and his eyes lit on something that made the blood pound in his veins. Rising from the garden that was beginning to have a broken-down look of its own was the yellow cage.

"Mother! What are you doing?"

"I asked the handyman to put it out," Ayela Linde replied, keeping to herself that she was merely obeying the cage's renewed and benevolent pull on her, that after all this time she was ready for it, or it for her. "Lord knows why I ever bought such a thing. Its history, I suppose," she said, and began to relate the provenance of the cage.

Her son cut her off. "I've got to get back to Boston tomorrow, and you've got to pack up the house. We can't have some piece of junk sitting out here!" He began to feel the old suffocation of this place, of the woman who was his mother, her willfulness, her unpredictability, and it made him wish to be anywhere but here.

Ayela Linde sat rigidly in her chair, wishing to God her sons had never given her a thought. Finally she stood up. "Kindly have the decency to allow me to do as I wish in my own house while it is still mine," she told her son, and with the air of an injured queen, turned and strode inside.

Xavier heard her moving about, tidying up, switching off lights. Just as he was about to beg her forgiveness for this entire debacle, she pulled the switch on the colored lanterns that lit the terrace, leaving her son in darkness.

He plunked himself down on the chaise lounge. It wasn't the white wicker he remembered, but yellow plastic, which saddened him and made him hotter, as did the thought of the stifling bedroom awaiting him under the eaves at the front of the house. "Damn," he said out loud. "Damn the heat. Damn her. Who doesn't have air-conditioning in this day and age!"

The words slid like stones into his mother's particular brand of punishing silence. Xavier Linde began to swig his tequila, recognizing himself, once again, as the victim of grave injustice from day one. He bowed his head, grieving for that small boy who, because he'd watched his mother watering with a garden hose, took his penis out of his short pants to water the flowers alongside her, and was sent to his room without dinner, suffering less from her harsh sentence than from knowing in his child's heart that his help had only angered his mother. Deep in his cells he had always known his mother had loved his brother Freddie better than he and then the youngest, Jesse, better than both of them, despite what his father had always maintained: that by the time her thirdborn came along, Ayela Linde had finally gotten the hang of motherhood.

Xavier Linde let loose with a loud tequila belch. "Shit," he muttered and cursed himself for his own self-pity, for making this visit in the summer, for making it at all, and, alone in the dark terrace in the smothering heat, he thought he might cry.

After the departure of her son, Ayela Linde tried to ignore of the idea of a future in Boston. The Linde house was built in the last century. Its large formal rooms with ceiling fans, the black-and-white marble foyer flanked by two reception areas, a courtyard with a columned arcade where the boys played horseshoes and Frederick held his chamber music evenings and where Concha now grew her pots of verbena, prompted Ayela Linde to observe, "The buyer will have second thoughts. People don't live this way anymore."

She floated along on this cloud of delusion until a Thursday afternoon three weeks later. Concha had fallen asleep on the terrace, and still dressed in her night clothes, Ayela Linde answered the door.

"Hello again." Mr. Aguilera bowed, avoiding her eyes. "Your son asked me to come . . ."

"My son has gone back to Boston," Ayela Linde replied, without inviting him inside.

"But the house must be completely emptied . . . ," he went on.

"Yes," she cut him off, fully aware that her reign as mistress of this house ended in sixty days, when the new owners took possession.

Mr. Aguilera bowed his head. The house seemed sadder than he remembered and leaning toward decrepitude, led by the two stone lions that stood sentinel on the front portico, one of which had lost its back leg, the other its head. When he looked up again it was with apology in his eyes.

Ayela Linde blushed.

Hers was the most comfortable house in creation. But the truth was that she and Concha were collapsing from the weight of it, from the missing flagstones and the sagging tiled roof and the dusty stucco and the emptiness of the formal rooms and all the other thousands of unanswered groans. The grand old house was losing ground, just like the two of them.

"Well then," he said. "Let's begin where we left off. In the storeroom."

With a steady look, she searched his face. Slowly she unfastened the key from the chain around her neck and handed it to him.

"I'll be quick," he said.

"There's no hurry. Take all year if you want," she replied, leading him through the house out the back door to the storeroom.

He stopped her in front of the garden, and spoke to her gently. "And after the storeroom, I'll have to take a look at the house."

Ayela Linde sighed. "Look wherever you like," she said. "But you'll have to excuse me." With the sense that something very dear to her was coming to an end, she left him and retreated upstairs to throw herself down on her bed.

Frederick had ordered the king-size bed when those things first became available, when they hadn't needed it because they still slept with their arms around each other. She'd teased him about it, but over the years it had proven a wise investment as they gradually and without rancor pulled away into themselves, sleeping as close to their own edge as possible, in reach of their own night table piled with books and spectacles and pills.

Concha first slept with her in the conjugal bed a year ago last fall. "Your cold is trapped inside your head," Concha told her, nursing her with eucalyptus oil and gentle massages of the frontal and maxillary sinuses and staying with her to supply the comforting presence of health in the sickbed. They slept in the same bed first out of necessity, then because they couldn't go on any other way.

"Dear Concha," she murmured, and, lying on her back in the middle of the bed, Ayela Linde thought in a rational way about what time held for the two of them. She could see more difficulty in moving their ancient bowels, more insomniac nights, the infernal shakes, the fracture of brittle bones, two shrinking women content to remain in their nightclothes for weeks. Desire to have a body would cease. Then would come the endless days of being a burden to themselves and everyone else, left to thieving and disinterested nurses who would bathe them and change their diapers and put them to bed until they finally submitted to the will of God. She dared not pose the horrifying question of which one would be the first to submit.

Ayela Linde lay quietly, vaguely aware of the footsteps up and down the stairs, the softening sun, the faraway voices of Mr. Aguilera and Concha, then the closing of the heavy front door.

It was nearing dark when she awoke from her thoughts. Had the seed not been planted, the revelation might have never seized her by the throat and dragged her down the road of reason. But, alone on the bed in which two of her three sons had been conceived, she had come to understand: "Bless you, Xavier," she whispered.

She went to Frederick's library to wait for the call she knew was coming. When it came, the bid for the contents of the house was not generous, she could have held out, counter offered, pled unfairness. The bid was not generous, but it was reasonable, and in the past day Ayela Linde had become gloriously reasonable.

She said nothing about the offer, but as a lawyer's wife was aware of the business to be done, and the following morning, wearing a simple dress of pale linen, she drove to the office of Mr. Aguilera to sign the papers with the eagerness of a girl on summer holiday.

Two nights later, Concha sat with pillows propped up behind her, the tiny black transistor radio on her lap and the earplug in her right ear when Ayela Linde came into the bedroom with two bowls. "I've made the banana pudding you like," she announced.

Concha's dentures were already soaking in the glass on the night table, and in response she could only grin the gummy smile of a newborn.

The hour was late and they ate without speaking. The only sound was the scraping of spoon against bowl, and when they were done Ayela Linde put the bowls on a white lacquer tray that was waiting on the dresser.

In the immense bed, Ayela Linde reached across the expanse of sheet and took Concha's hand in hers. The hand was small, like a child's though far more knowing, and smelling faintly of lemon. Ayela Linde pressed it to her cheek and closed her eyes. "Such hands," she whispered, and gently let it drop on the bed. She smiled at Concha: "Get some rest now."

Concha lay her head back on the pillow and let her eyelids drop. Ayela Linde watched her and did not shift her gaze until Concha fell asleep, then she gently lifted the earplug from her ear and put the radio on the nightstand, watching like an angel of mercy until Concha's breath turned low and even, and then ceased.

Only then did Ayela lie back. Dressed in the pale blue nightdress she had worn since the early days of her marriage, she gave herself over to the strange torpor that had begun to envelop her at the last taste of the pudding. She opened her mouth as if to say something. But what came out was a single sound, shrill and joyous, like the song of a jungle bird.

16
Dreaming of You
2004

Did you ever wake from the muddled heap of events that is your life, stir from the paths you have taken, and know that they are all wrong? That a dream you have had for many months, years, is now what you should take hold of, and it is as unmistakable and tantalizingly clear as your own image in a mountain lake? Have you ever felt that a matter of urgency was passing you by, that you were connected to it by a thread, just a thread that was becoming weaker and more frayed by the minute, and if you didn't recover, sit up and splash your face with cold water, and grab on to it that very instant, that, well, something irreplaceable would vanish from your life?

I have been dreaming of her my whole life. My Nana Santa Rosalia.

Dreaming of her because I never got enough of her. Because she was there and I was here. Such little time we had together. Yet every moment cherished, remembered in full and tucked away in a little blue velvet box in the corner of my mind.

I am the daughter of her second son, Freddie, and they say I look like her. All of them say so, Father, Uncle Xavier, and Uncle Jesse, even Mother. "The resemblance is too strong for your own good," Father says with a laugh.

That delights me.

The shining dark hair, the olive eyes, the impertinent yet tender mouth, the voluptuous dark beauty. Can that be me?

"No one else in the family got her looks," Mother says. "Not even her own boys. It's as if she saved them all up for you."

Yes, the looks, all fine and good. But you see, there's much more to it than that.

Do you believe people can speak to you from beyond the grave?

I'm convinced of it.

And when they call, you'd better pay attention.

She died five years ago, and with each passing month the calls get stronger. This is what she does: she insinuates herself into my thoughts and elbows her way front and center. Secretly, I thank her, my Nana Santa Rosalia, so romantic, so far away, her Mexican ways so mysterious, so unlike the tenor of my life. And me, her special one, she reminds me. Her *muchacha bonita*. Sending me presents when I was a girl on odd holidays, the Feast of Christ the King, the summer equinox, the Day of the Dead. Even the wrappings, unlike any I knew, bright packages tied in raffia. Inside, a fringed silk shawl, a Mexican lace dress, blood oranges, the pencil drawing of a guinea hen. And her letters. She wrote on thin blue sheets of airmail paper, so fragile they might turn to dust with the weight of my eyes passing over the words. Writing faithfully, but never coming to see us in Boston after that first time, that bitter cold January. She came dressed in a shawl and open-toed shoes. "The cold is not for me," she said, and wore Papa's flannel bathrobe and woolen socks around the house for the rest of the trip and refused to go out.

"It's too cold for me up there, in more ways than one," she liked to say.

"Oh, come on, Mother, don't be such a snob," Father would chide her, but she did not visit us again. It was left to us to go south, to her magical Santa Rosalia, to the white house that smelled of roses, with the whirring ceiling fans and the fish-mouth faucets and the orange tile floors and the chimes tinkling in the garden. Heaven. We went, but there were never enough visits to her, never enough opportunities to drink in the gorgeous soul of her, her beautiful wild dresses, the moonstone earrings, her proud face. She made me think of a black horse galloping alone through a field, faster than the other horses could imagine, galloping just to gallop. And, there, you see, that is what she does to me.

Nana Santa Rosalia called to me that June evening, a dreaded Saturday evening, the ordeal of cocktails and dinner at Nana Boston's, the other one's eighty-fifth birthday.

Nana Santa Rosalia and Nana Boston. That's what we called our grandmothers, among ourselves anyway. Designated by where they came from, but that said it all. Boston.

Such a cold, clipped word, just like Nana Boston. So tall and thin and pinched and loaded, something about her that made us want to make faces and curse and act up in front of her though at the same time we were mortally afraid that we might do or say the wrong thing in her presence.

An early June evening for the party at the house on Louisburg Square. One of the loveliest on Beacon Hill, and Greek Revival, as Nana Boston never tires of telling us.

Mother had insisted or I would never have gone. None of us would have. But there we were on the doorstep, right on time.

"Note the frieze with its row of distinctive Greek triglyph ornament," says Father.

"Be nice, Freddie," says Mother. "This is the house I grew up in, after all."

"Note the cornice with its display of a row of toothlike dentil molding," parrots my younger sister Isabel.

"Note the hundred bluebloods milling about, falling over each other to grab drinks from the waiters with the silver trays," I say.

Mother laughs. "I know, I know, but please be nice!"

"Ah, the Lindes have arrived," cried Ann North, Mother's sister's girl, as we stepped into the foyer. "Cousin Leyla! What's the matter? You look so glum."

Ann North, looking ravishing, as blondes do in black. She is only twenty-two, nearly ten years younger than I, though she always manages to take the upper hand with me.

And Nana Boston right behind her. "She's always unhappy, our little artist, isn't she?" Nana Boston cooed and pecked my cheek. "You're stressed, isn't that what they say nowadays? You must come out to Greensport this summer and relax."

"Yes, of course, Nana." I let myself be kissed. "Happy birthday."

The crush of more arrivals, more greetings, more adulation, and me carried along like a piece of driftwood, exiled to a clear pool in the middle of the room.

I felt a hand on my shoulder.

It was Uncle Xavier, the old dear, Father's older brother. "I'm so happy to see you!" I hugged him.

Uncle Xavier chuckled. "Your mother wangled me an invitation. She couldn't bear to let me miss the social event of the season."

"Right, no one should ever miss a Nana Boston celebration."

He looked sideways at me. "The old girl gotten to you already?"

"Oh, I was just thinking."

"That's dangerous, you know."

We both laughed, then recovered.

Uncle Xavier waited politely for me to speak.

"God. How did my mother ever stand her?"

"Ah," he said. "We stand a great many things from our mothers."

He gave a signal for a waiter to bring us drinks.

"Not from *your* mother, though. Not from Nana Santa Rosalia."

Xavier smiled. "Yes, from my mother."

"I miss her very much, you know."

"But did you spend so much time with her? I hadn't thought you did."

"No, that's true," I admitted woefully, adding petulantly that the grandchildren hadn't even been allowed to go to the funeral!

Uncle Xavier sighed and shook his head. "Her death, you know, and Concha's, a bad business all around."

"It was an accident. A simple accident. That's what Father thinks."

"Well, it was so . . . strange, really. If it had been an accident, there would have been . . . well . . . they wouldn't have been found upstairs . . . in the bed, now, would they? Oh, who can say, really. Those two old women rattling around that house, who knows what went on. We should never have allowed it."

"I don't care, I loved her anyway," I blurted. "Didn't you?"

"Love?" Uncle Xavier hesitated. "I don't know if I'd call it that."

"But of course you would!" Uncle Xavier sipped his drink and looked away. His voice lost its politeness. "I don't think she really ever liked me," he said bitterly. "I think she thought I was pathetic."

"Uncle Xavier, you are no such thing!" I threw my arms around him. What a tactless baboon I was.

"So sorry," I murmured into him, "so sorry." Uncle Xavier's frame was thinner than Father's, and slightly bent, like an old man's, and I hugged him tighter because of it and because I did know deep down that Nana Santa Rosalia had preferred my own father to Uncle Xavier, and Uncle Jesse to both of them, for his looks and temperament and irreverent spirit that most closely coincided with her own. That kind of favoritism hurt Uncle Jesse, just as it hurt me, the favorite among the grandchildren, hurt us because it hurt the others, and it spoiled things for us too, knowing that the light of her smile falling only on us was for the obvious and contemptible reason that we reminded her of herself. Still, I loved her madly, or at least the idea of her.

"Look who's here!" cried Ann North, interrupting us to show off her brother Dickie, who was a stockbroker in New York.

"I've deserted Wall Street for the occasion," said Dickie, beaming. "So you know it's got to be important."

Uncle Xavier winked at me.

"How's the art biz, Leyla?" inquired Dickie with a sly grin.

"Well, unproductive, as usual." I tried to sound nonchalant.

"Let's see, how long has that been going on now?" he pressed me.

"Oh, about a hundred years," I replied, hoping for comic relief.

Ann North shot her brother a "shut up" look.

Uncle Xavier came to my rescue. "It's painting," he said rather sternly. "Not planting potatoes," he said, "or selling shoe polish."

"Touché. You got my number, Uncle Xavier." Dickie laughed with surprising good grace. "I'm just a potato planter in the halls of commerce."

To everyone's relief, Ann North called over Jenna Barnes and Lanie Menkel.

There was talk of a summer at the Cape. Jenna and Lanie were taking a house with some friends.

"But it's so touristy," Ann North complained.

"It's touristy everywhere now," Dickie agreed.

"It's true," Lanie Menkel said. "I'm tempted to stay in the movie theater all summer. Just see one film after another."

Dickie North howled. "You're a card!" he said to Lanie.

More wine. And funny little pancakes for hors d'oeuvres.

Nana Santa Rosalia, I have to laugh at her, the old fox. Doesn't she just know when I'm most susceptible to her charms, that when I am in the company of the other, of Nana Boston and her ilk, is the best time to strike, and to deluge me with memories.

As Dickie and Lanie and the rest of them prattled on, Nana Santa Rosalia came calling. First it was the Spanish doll with red high heels and flouncy skirts and castanets she gave me when we arrived in Santa Rosalia. Then, how I loved to open the door to her closet full of sparkling, spangly dresses made by her own mother in every color in the garden, letting me touch the satin, the tulle, the organdy, the bows and beads, telling me their stories, calling each dress by a name, Soledad, Corazón, Isabel, Margarita. And then this: the poor child crying her head off because Mother forbade her to play in the puddles for fear of ruining her dress before the party. Nana Santa Rosalia pulled the tearstained

girl on her lap. "Well," she said. "What Mother says, goes.
But let's see what washed in with the rain." She led the girl
to the kitchen where hundreds of beautiful little cakes and
candies stood in their beauty, all shaped like flowers and
fishes and stars and fruits. My whole body trembled with
excitement and I began to jump up and down. "Come on,"
she said. "Help me arrange them. And I'm not expecting
that they'll all make it to the party."

"Leyla!" Dickie North waved his hand in front of my face.
"Earth to Leyla."

"Oh, sorry, I didn't know you were talking to me."

"Where are you tonight, dear?" Ann North said.

"Definitely not here," said Dickie with some disgust.
"Hey, I wanted to tell you about an opening I went to in
New York the other night. Alina Malesovich. Does this in-
teractive sculpture thing. Totally amazing. She sold every
piece opening night. Thought you might know her."

"No. Sorry. I don't know anyone that successful," I said.

"Oooh, busted!" Dickie cried and went off into a fit of
obnoxious giggles.

Fortunately, Lanie Menkel's grandmother came over to
talk to him. "Buy me a drink, will you, Dickie dear?" she
purred. "I have some gossip for you." She took his arm and
the two of them walked off together.

The cake, the birthday cake; people were beginning to
talk about it, saying it was spectacular. Ann North claimed
to have seen it. Aunt Carolyn, Ann's mother, said it came
from Douquet's. My mother said it had been flown in from

London and that it was to be displayed only after the sun had set. That piece of information astounded Ann North.

She grabbed me by the arm. "Just look at all this, Leyla, these people. Our people. Isn't this the best!" In a fit of high inspiration she pulled me along to spread the word about the birthday cake to each and every person in the room.

I let myself be trotted about, smiling, nodding, following Ann North's lead until I could no longer feign interest in a birthday cake or Nana Boston or reaching the age of eighty-five. Along the way, I felt a daring course of action mounting in me, an answer to Nana Santa Rosalia's call.

Around eight o'clock I extricated myself from Ann North. The party was in full swing, the brittle, overdesigned light making everybody look a little more horrid than they actually were. It took me quite a while to locate Mother to tell her that I needed some air and was leaving. "I wish I could go with you," she whispered, and kissed me good-bye, resigning herself to receiving the spiel being delivered by her second cousin on the genealogy of the family as far back as the Massachusetts Bay Colony.

Before anyone could stop me, I made a beeline for the kitchen, which had been taken over by the legions of caterers and cooks and assistants and bartenders and waiters, all rushing about, and, waiting to see that no one was watching, ran out through the back door like a thief.

The puddle jumper down to Santa Rosalia was smaller than I remembered, and when I boarded I felt the stares of all fourteen passengers. Why wouldn't they stare? Me with my smudged mascara, stiletto heels, and chandelier earrings at ten o'clock in the morning. My hair all disheveled, my fuchsia dress wrinkled like I'd slept in it, which I had, for four hours on an orange plastic chair in the middle of the night at the Atlanta airport. Eyes on the floor, I squeezed down the aisle to my seat at the back of the plane, clutching tightly to my weekend bag, the one thing that kept me from appearing a total vagabond. I sat down, holding the bag on my lap, saying a silent prayer of thanks for it and the one moment of practicality last night in which I raced by my apartment for a few essentials. Fortunately, no one could see what essentials the bag contained: old letters from Nana Santa Rosalia, her wedding picture, my paints, two favorite brushes, an assortment of sketchpads, a silk shawl, a package of Fig Newtons, and a knot of mismatched clothes from the laundry hamper.

I was still holding fast to the weekend bag when I finally arrived in Santa Rosalia and stood facing the desk clerk at the Hotel del Norte.

He gave me that same what-are-you-doing-here stare that the airline passengers had. "How long will you be staying?" he asked dryly.

I had no answer for him.

"How long will you be here?" he repeated.

"I don't know. Oh. Well, let's say three days for starters then."

He gave me a look. "Okay." Then he handed me the room key without bothering to say anything further.

"My grandparents lived in Santa Rosalia," I said. "Did you know them?"

"I doubt it."

"They were . . . well, they were quite prominent in this town. My grandfather started the Arts Pavilion."

"The what?"

I repeated myself.

The clerk shuffled through the register. "I'm afraid I don't know the Arts Pavilion or your grandparents," he said without changing his bored expression, so I stopped and accepted the keys and climbed the stairs to my room, which looked onto a back courtyard planted with lemon trees around its periphery. Cats were asleep under the flowering bushes. A woman with a kerchief on her head was washing pots in the little fountain.

I'm going to like this place, I said to myself.

I bought some jeans and a secondhand bike. I wanted to go slowly, savor the town, seek out the stories I've heard since birth, remember. Sit in the square beneath the palms where Papa first set eyes on Nana Santa Rosalia. Walk down the crooked street of Felidia Garzón's dress store, discover all the things I heard about, dreamed about. Eagerly I set out, but it wasn't long before the inevitable disappointment took hold.

Can you imagine this? A market square, the flower sellers, parakeets in wooden cages, nougats piled high in a pyramid shape, women in cotton dresses buying oranges, children chasing each other in the sun, a few men loitering under the sabal palms smoking cigarettes, green jays, a young boy looking through the detective novels. You know that this is a small town, that people live and die here without having been ten miles away, that the bell calls them to a church that changes from quiet and cool to excruciatingly hot on Sunday as the congregants breathe heavily and close their eyes as the ancient priest rambles on about his pet theory of the Holy Ghost. That dress shop with the floaty green chiffon in the window and ladies stopping to stare and imagine, couples dancing on the outdoor dance floor at the pool hall, the mayor letting loose with a deluge of paper flowers over the crowd, somewhere a beautiful lady in an ivory dress with a diadem on her forehead, politicians steaming into town in their boats of a car and the people thronging the square to hear, listening with one heart. Life so thick and close you could cut it with a butter knife. So vivid, like a window to another world, a window one could step right through.

Riding the bike up and down the streets, there was nothing in evidence that I remembered or imagined I remembered. No flower stalls, no bird sellers, no makers of paper flowers, no ladies in gowns. Only a main street with ordinary stores. A hardware store. A beauty salon. A clothing store. A fast-food restaurant. A woman walked by holding the hand of her little boy. "No, you can't have a Big Mac now," she said to him in an unfriendly way. A teenage girl stood outside the grocery store talking on her cell phone. People rushing along, cavernous distances between them, just like anywhere else. All wrong. Life so thin and dull it slips through the hands like dust.

Was there anyone here who would have known her?

Showing the old snapshot of her would have been futile. Would the girl with the cell phone have known her? The woman cutting hair in the Silver Scissors Beauty Salon?

The policeman speaking into his walkie-talkie? The answer was already clear. No one knew Ayela Linde here. She was too old, belonged to another world, couldn't have existed like this.

I wanted to scream at Nana Santa Rosalia: What fool mission have you brought me on? What gives you the right to drag me here to this town that is ugly and dreary and heartbreaking in its normalcy, and bereft of you?

Sitting down on a bench in the square, my head in my hands, I silently ranted at her, expecting a response in return, some sign of acknowledgment, a hint of further direction. What came back to me was nothing, no memories, no inspiration of any kind. Nana Santa Rosalia had become maddeningly uncommunicative.

The square was deserted but for an old woman reading the newspaper. It was littered with trash. Leaves and a plastic bottle or two bobbed in the pool of the tired-looking tiered fountain, and the whole place smelled like dog.

"Damn it," I swore out loud and announced to a gray-and-white pigeon picking his way through a pack of discarded crackers, "I'm going home."

I couldn't leave without at least seeing Olivea Road. I wasn't expecting the shade. Though it had always been there when we drove up the road to Nana Santa Rosalia's, even as a child. The luxuriance of it. Shade from the trees on either side covering the street, protecting it. Completely still, and marvelous to be there, on the street of well-kept houses of an older vintage, a Spanish influence.

When you return somewhere, sometimes it is important not to look too closely. A glance, a quick one, will do nicely. A once-over and then head for the hills, for anything more may bring you face-to-face with ruination.

The neighborhood seemed run-down. Dirty plastic toys were strewn about the front lawns of the houses on Olivea Road, a beat-up car in that one's drive, a motorcycle on this one's porch. And then almost at the end, Nana Santa Rosalia's house. Smaller and less grand than I remembered, tarnished around the edges, in need of a face-lift, paint peeling off the white stucco. The rock garden by the wall gone. The paws of the headless lions guarding the front door eroded. A minivan with a side dent parked in the steep drive.

Was it right or wrong to have come here? Expecting what? Hoping for something that no one believes in any longer? But what do dreams have to do with anyone else, aren't they our own private consolations?

I stopped in front of Nana Santa Rosalia's house and sat on my bicycle.

A woman passed by on the street. She was wearing a pink sweatsuit and sneakers.

"Do you know the owners?" I nodded toward the house.

"Not yet. They just moved in last month."

"Oh. Well, maybe you remember my grandmother. She lived here once," I told her. "Maybe you knew her. Ayela Linde."

The woman thought for a minute. "No. We only moved here a few years ago."

"There were two of them. Older ladies. Every now and

then they'd string the house with colored lights and invite the neighborhood. They loved to cook. The food was something! Don't you remember at least hearing about them?"

She shook her head. "No, dear, I don't. Sorry. And I would have remembered something like that."

I thanked her for that, and she walked on, leaving me face-to-face with the old house. I turned away and broke into a fast ride on my bike, standing up to pedal harder and harder down Olivea Road until I was far from it, far from the town, past the used-car dealers, past the discount stores, past the fields, almost to the citrus groves. I threw down my bike and lay on the grass, face first.

The tears came.

I should have known, and maybe I did.

In Santa Rosalia nothing remained of Ayela and Frederick Linde.

They were like stones that had been thrown into a lake and swallowed whole, the ripples had come and gone, smoothed out, leaving the lake glassy and undisturbed.

As if the stones had never been thrown.

As if they had never existed.

Then how to explain what happened? Days of ranting at Nana: How could your glorious stories have come from this awful little town? Did they ever really happen? Did I hear them correctly? And lamenting that her loveliness had been swallowed by the past. Lamenting that she's gone, her time has gone, its beauty degenerated into this insipid, ugly, inelegant life. Then gradually, after the first week in Santa Rosalia, my resistance fading, and in its place a new softness, a yielding to a routine of odd, insignificant activity that took on frightening significance, working in peculiar and inexplicable ways to bring about what I had dreamed of. Waking to the laughter of the chambermaids in the courtyard. Taking an early breakfast, solo in the hotel dining room, to hear Severina, the waitress from the Yucatan, sing to herself as she set the rest of the tables. Sitting in the first pew of the Church of San Lorenzo, to witness the faces of the old women, worn with devotion, tending to the altar. Ambling through the stores, the market, chatting with the old man who ran the newsstand, bicycling out to the small cemetery to have a sandwich and cold tea in the presence of Nana and Papa Santa Rosalia under the tall shade trees and the umbrella of unnatural quiet. Then in the early afternoons, too hot and humid for anything but a nap, returning to the Hotel del Norte, closing the curtains and drinking in the scent of roses from the bouquet I bought daily, falling into a hard sleep until the hottest part of the day had passed.

The days were for searching and sleeping, but the evenings, with their light and cooler air, they were for working. The evening light had claimed me from my first night in Santa Rosalia. A soft glow, inviting and clear, that turned to a shade of rose-gold I'd never seen and generously stayed so until the sun went down. Each evening I sat in the square, feeling its pull until resistance was futile. There was the initial self-consciousness of it, working out in the open. Then the reassuring routine of it, every evening after dinner the two-block walk from the Hotel del Norte to the square, taking the bench facing the bell tower. Nana's square, the crowded, gossipy square full of men with slicked-back hair eyeing girls in flouncy dresses. Now dismally seedy, a forgotten place, trash-strewn and run-down. Crossed by rough-looking, dope-smoking teenagers. Inhabited in the evenings by two old women, inmates of the rest home by the church, dressed in their hospital gowns, waiting, waiting, on their broken bench, and calling in vain to the dog licking at the dirty fountain water.

First the small pencil drawings on a little pad. Unsure, silly, desperate attempts to record a shard of the truth of Nana Santa Rosalia, the tilt of her head, the sheen of her hair. Then the paints, the canvas, the easel I bought in town, and with them the termination of thought that brought work in a steady, unblinking blur. Scenes emerging on the canvas, coming at such a clip, seeming to fall from my brush, knowing that there was only time to rough it out before another struggled to come forward. A man watching a girl in a rose-colored summer dress in this very square. The square immaculate, and in the midst of it, the parasols, scattered this way and that. A woman dressed in an ivory gown, a diadem at her forehead. A little band of mourners praying over a grave, roses growing up all around them. An old woman bent over her sewing surrounded by floating dresses of sea foam green, coral, whisper pink. A figure in flowing robes locked in a fanciful yellow cage. A young boy with the wings of a phoenix. A man and woman facing different ways on the back of a cow in the rain.

These were my evenings, dream evenings I never imagined possible, and all compliments of my Nana Santa Rosalia. So precious, these evenings in the square amidst my companions, the two ladies from the rest home, the little boy floating leaf boats in the dirty fountain, the woman who brought me sponge cake soaked in rosewater so she could watch me paint. The rose-gold light. And the paintings, so many after all this time, and the gratitude for that, but for far more than that. For the peace in my heart. For the feeling of being out of time, beyond the tyranny of thought, wholly alone, and yet, for a moment, possessed of the expansive grace that ties one to all creatures.